THE SIGNAL

THE MULTIVERSE CHRONICLES

NICK COOK

ABOUT THE AUTHOR

Somewhere back in the mists of time, Nick was born in the great sprawling metropolis of London. He grew up in a family where art was always a huge influence. Tapping into this, Nick finished college with a fine art degree tucked into his back pocket. Faced with the prospect of actually trying to make a living from his talents, he plunged into the emerging video game industry back in the eighties. It was the start of a long career and he produced graphics for many of the top-selling games on the early home computers, including *Aliens* and *Enduro Racer*. Those pioneering games may look crude now, but back then they were considered to be cutting edge. As the industry exploded into the one we know today, Nick's career went supernova. He worked on titles such as *X-Com*, and set up two studios, which produced

Warzone 2100 and the *Conflict: Desert Storm* series. He has around forty published titles to his name.

As great as the video game industry is, a little voice kept nagging inside Nick's head, and at the end of 2006 he was finally ready to pursue his other passion as a full-time career: writing. Many years later, he completed his first trilogy, *Cloud Riders*. And the rest, as they say, is history.

Nick has many interests, from space exploration and astronomy to travelling the world. He has flown light aircraft and microlights, an experience he used as research for *Cloud Riders*. He's always loved to cook, but then you'd expect it with his surname. His writing in many ways reflects his own curiosity about the world around him. He loves to let his imagination run riot to pose the question: *What if?*

ALSO BY NICK COOK

Prequel to the Multiverse Chronicles

The Earth Song Series (The Multiverse Chronicles)

The Fractured Light Trilogy (The Multiverse Chronicles)

I will always owe a huge debt of thanks to the Lair of Lost Authors for encouraging me to write this.

'Somewhere, something incredible is waiting to be known.'
Carl Sagan

CHAPTER ONE

OUTSIDE, the hulking presence of our Lovell radio telescope was picked out by spotlights against the night sky. Just past 2 a.m., it was currently aimed low towards an unseen target near the eastern horizon: a distant black hole that I knew we were capturing data from for an astrophysics team back at Manchester University.

With my arms loaded up, I pushed the door open with my hip and entered the 1950s-retro-styled control room of Jodrell Bank.

On the control panels, the readout displays showed a series of sine-wave peaks and troughs rolling into our systems courtesy of Lovell's giant metal bowl.

Steve turned his attention from his laptop. It looked as if he was watching the original *War of the Worlds* movie, probably to kill the tedium of his graveyard shift.

With a broad smile I swung round to reveal the ridiculously monstrous pizza box between my arms. 'Ta-da!'

Steve took in the 'Mario's' logo on the box and shook his head.

'Now that's one serious bribe, Lauren Stelleck. Who spilt the beans about my all-time favourite pizza restaurant?'

'Hey, I have friends in high places,' I replied.

'In other words, you've been talking to Graham again, haven't you?'

I grinned. 'Absolutely. Anyway, that's not the real bribe.' I placed the box down on a table as I unhitched my rucksack from my back. 'If it's bribes you're after, then check this out.' I withdrew a parcel wrapped with star constellation paper that I'd grabbed from the gift shop in our visitor centre.

I dipped my head and raised my arms up towards Steve with the parcel. 'This is your gift, oh wonderful one with a heart of gold.'

He hitched an eyebrow at me as he started to unwrap the present. A few rips later he was holding a *Millennium Falcon* Star Wars T-shirt in his hands. 'OK, due kudos, Lauren; this is very cool.'

'I know it is, although I did get into something of a bidding war on eBay for it. It's an original collector's item but it was worth the price. Graham said you'd love it.'

Steve placed a hand over his heart. 'I am, and always will be, an eternal Star Wars geek, so yes absolutely. But you really shouldn't have.'

'Oh, but I so should, because I do have ulterior motives.'

Steve snorted. 'Of course you do.'

A soft chime came from the console and he glanced across at it.

'All good?' I asked.

'Yes, the system has just finished capturing the first data run for NGC 1277, which should keep the team at Manchester happy for a while. Next, I need to recalibrate the sensors for a second run, but we can squeeze in your project now if you like?'

I tipped my head to one side. 'How did you know?'

He gestured towards the pizza and his new T-shirt.

I laughed. 'Busted. But you're sure it's OK? Because I know how tight telescope time is at the moment with everyone's projects stacked up back to back.'

'Our schedule may be fit to bursting, but for you, Lauren, anything. However, I will have to swear you to secrecy. We don't want the Manchester team coming after me with their proverbial pitchforks.'

I smiled at Steve, enjoying the image of the angry mob of astronomy academics pursuing me across the Cheshire countryside. 'It will be our little secret. Anyway, where's Phil? I thought he was meant to be working with you tonight?'

'My partner in crime cried off earlier when he phoned in with an Oscar-worthy hacking cough performance to convince me of his dreadful state of health.'

'Not like him, especially when it's movie night.'

Steve just shrugged. 'Probably his poker night that no one here is meant to know about.'

'I guess that's his idea of a good time.' I tapped the top of one of the computer speakers. 'So do you mind if I have a listen in to what you've captured already?'

'Knock yourself out.'

'Great.' I reached across and turned the volume up on my speakers as I sat down.

At once rising and falling crackling sounds filled the control room. I leant back in my chair and gazed off into empty air as a trance-like state took hold of me.

I breathed in the slightly musty air of the control room. Even though I wasn't looking at him, I could sense Steve watching me with the slight wide-eyed look he always had when he knew that I was tuning in to my synaesthesia, something that he and everyone else always found endlessly fascinating.

I ignored him and focused my attention on the light patterns dancing to the beat of static that were now superimposed over my view of the control room. These patterns of light were always there for me to a greater or lesser extent, but certain audio sources, such as the one I was listening to now, turned those sounds into my very own personal disco light show.

I remember the first time I realised my gift as if it was yesterday. I'd been five years old, visiting the Science Museum in London with Aunt Lucy, when we'd discovered the exhibit about the life cycle of stars. I'd stood, hypnotised, as I listened to the clicks and whirs of a pulsar that had triggered a symphony of vision in my eyes.

Steve leant forward. 'What are you seeing, Lauren? Can you describe it?'

Describing my own version of reality was always something of a challenge – the equivalent of trying to explain to someone who was blind what sight was like.

'Imagine the most incredible firework display made from overlapping shapes and points of light, all dancing over each other and ranging from reds to blues, then you'd be getting reasonably close,' I said.

He shook his head. 'I'll never be able to get my head around the fact that you can see sounds in this way.'

'And I will never get my head around the fact that most other people can't. It's part of who I am as much as my sense of smell and my hearing.'

Steve slowly nodded. 'So when did you first realise you weren't like the other pesky kids? That you were "special"?' He added air quotes to that final word.

I gave him an eye-roll. 'For your information, Steve, I was about six when I finally figured out that other people couldn't see the world in the same way that I could. My parents freaked out at first but relaxed when a specialist told them that I had synaesthesia.'

Steve offered me his bucket of popcorn. 'Still, it must be strange to be in your shoes, right?'

I grabbed a handful of the proffered snack. 'Not really. You have to remember that this has always been my normal. I also have some pretty famous company to hang out with. Both David Hockney and Kandinsky were well known to be synaesthetes. I actually feel sorry for the rest of you who don't get to see the world like I do.'

'We poor mortals, hey?'

'Something like that. However...' I opened the pizza box and acted out wafting the scent towards him. 'Breathe deeply, Steve – pepperoni and anchovy, your favourite.'

He shook his head. 'You so know how to push my buttons, Lauren. OK, so what's your target for tonight's deliberation?'

I beamed at him and pulled out my phone from my rucksack, which of course was already in flight mode. From the moment anyone stepped on to the Jodrell Bank site there were numerous signs displayed reminding them to keep their phones switched off, or as in my case in flight mode. The problem was that our radio telescopes were so sensitive, designed as they were to pick up the radio signal equivalent of a candle flame on the moon, that a single stray mobile phone signal to a cellular mast could totally screw with our data during a capture session.

I scrolled down the list of targets on my phone and selected the one I'd marked in bold text. 'Ah, here she is.' I handed my phone to him.

Steve's eyebrows crept up his forehead. 'My old friend J1925+1720, a possible supernova remnant, otherwise a fairly run-of-the-mill pulsar.'

'Hey, your unremarkable is my visual symphony.'

'If you say so. So why did you choose this particular target?'

I coughed. 'I used my free-form selection technique.'

'In other words, you ran your finger down a list with your eyes closed?'

I laughed. 'Busted again.' It might have been a random approach but that was part of the fun of this – I never knew what it would throw up with my synaesthesia.

Steve smiled and began typing at the keyboard.

I watched him search through the database with a growing sense of anticipation as he pulled up the coordinates for my pulsar.

He highlighted it and hit return. 'Your pulsar is locked and loaded.' He gestured towards the big button in the middle of the control console for the Lovell dish and nodded to me.

I stared at him. 'Seriously, you trust me to operate Lovell?'

'I think you've more than proved yourself as my go-to person, Lauren, and anyway, we're only talking about pushing a button.'

My heart actually fluttered because what that button did was the stuff of my dreams. Before Steve could change his mind, I leant forward and slammed my hand down hard on the control. At once an answering warble came from the console and, with a faint whine of motors, outside 1500 tons of steel bowl started to rotate towards my pulsar.

'You so never forget your first time,' Steve said with a grin.

I gave him the look.

He coughed and returned his attention to the display.

This was all part of our regular flirtation that never actually led anywhere. Though I really wasn't into Steve the way he obviously was into me. Plus I had a certain amount of experience that had taught me not to combine pleasure with work, like one of those dodgy blue cocktails that looked great at the bar but always left you with a brain-melting hangover.

Lovell's giant metal dish slowly rotated on its track as it pivoted towards its new target and my excitement grew to epic proportions.

An alarm shrieked out, accompanied by at least ten red warning lights. Lovell slowed to a complete stop and it felt as if someone had just cancelled Christmas and shot Rudolf for good measure.

'Damn and blast,' Steve muttered.

I raised my hands up from the console where I'd been resting them. 'That definitely was not me.'

'Relax, I know it wasn't, Lauren. According to the readings we've just had another power spike. I bet it's that right axial motor unit glitching out again. Of course the tech team was meant to have serviced that particular motor last week.'

'Timing, hey?'

'I know, but you can relax because everything should be OK once I've reset the breakers. However, that means a trip up to the engine room to sort this out. Fancy tagging along?'

'You mean I get to push the big button and climb to the summit all on the same night?'

'Why not? If we're going to initiate you we may as well go all in.'

I looked up through the window at Lovell and my stomach clenched slightly. As always it looked ridiculously high to climb.

'Fantastic,' I replied, trying to inject a note of extra-bright I'm-really-not-scared-to-death enthusiasm into my voice.

'We'll take the lift up most of the way.' He cast a glance towards the Mario's box. 'The only problem is that the pizza will be as cold as the cardboard it came in by the time we get back down here.'

I grabbed a slice and offered it to Steve. 'Who says you can't eat on the job?'

'Good point.' He took the slice and sunk his teeth in. A look of utter bliss filled his face. 'So good.'

I smiled at him. 'If I say so myself, I do know what makes you tick.'

He tossed me a head torch from his drawer and took one for himself. 'OK, temptress, let's get this show back on the road.'

The moment we stepped outside, the chill of the autumn-night air washed over my skin. But in reality I was only dimly aware of the temperature because my whole attention was focused on the beautiful monument to scientific endeavour standing before us.

Many might see the Lovell as an impressive piece of structural engineering that had taken five years to build back in the fifties. But for someone like me who could literally see sound, Lovell was like a love poem from humanity to the cosmos. Not that I would ever admit these thoughts to Steve or anyone else who worked here for fear of being branded a hopeless romantic. No, hard scientific thinking was what got you ahead in your job at a place like Jodrell Bank.

We cut across the public area under the flood of spotlights, chewing on our slices of pizza, and headed through the gate. As we walked beneath the giant metal bowl, easily the size of a football pitch, the usual sense of awe took hold. Lovell's charm would never fade for me.

Steve headed towards the nearest of two massive support legs and approached the door set into it. He pressed a button and then cast me a frown as he finished his pizza slice. 'That's strange. It looks like the power's been tripped to the lift system as well.'

'Why strange?'

'Because the lift system is on a separate circuit to the main ones for the whole reason that no one wants to use the alternative method to get up there when a maintenance check is needed.'

'Please tell that doesn't mean what I think it does?'

He nodded and gestured towards the series of ladders that snaked their way up the side of the leg we were standing beside. 'You really don't have to do this. It's a big enough rush of blood to the head walking out on to the gantry from the lift for the first time without throwing in a ten-minute climb as well.'

'A fear of heights is something you should face up to rather than let rule your life.'

'In that case...' He started up the ladder ahead of me.

With a mental equivalent of a breath I put my hand on the first rung and the cold of the metal bit into my palms. As I began the climb I had no idea that what would happen next was going to change the rest of my life for ever.

CHAPTER TWO

THE FIRST TEN metres of the ascent of Lovell were by far the worst and, despite the cold turning my hands to blocks of ice, I grew sweaty as I clung to the ladder.

Vertigo sucked.

Yet once we passed the second flight of ladders, already at the height of a house, the bitterness tainting the back of my mouth started to vanish. I was so high now that the effect of a fall was something of a moot point.

Rung by rung, metre by metre, I gradually became calmer as the night landscape began to reveal itself around us. Over the top of the trees the few distant lights of houses were dotted across the countryside. Further out, Macclesfield, our nearest city neigh-bour glowed orange on the horizon.

Above me, Steve started to hum 'Stairway to Heaven' as his head-torch beam danced over Lovell's metal latticework.

'Good tune choice,' I called up to him.

'It's something of a tradition for me. I find it helps keep me distracted.'

'From?'

'From my vomit-inducing fear of heights.'

'And there was me thinking it was only me. You've never said anything about it before.'

'Of course not, Lauren. Can you imagine the amount of piss-taking I'd be letting myself in for with the others?'

'Way too easily. So that will be another of our little secrets then.'

'And that right there is one of the reasons that I hired you – you are discretion personified.'

'Not on account of my academic brilliance and my perky disposition then?'

'Those things too.'

With Steve continuing to hum 'Stairway to Heaven' to himself we reached the gantry at last.

He shut his eyes for a moment as he gripped the rail and stepped out on to the gangway.

Through an act of pure willpower I managed to keep my legs from wobbling as I followed him along the walkway towards the door to the engine room, making sure to keep my eyes dead ahead.

Steve took out a key to unlock the door.

I'd no idea why they needed a lock up here. If a thief managed to make it all the way up here, then in my humble opinion they more than deserved their haul of copper wiring or whatever loot they were after.

We headed into the motor room. Inside, Steve's head-torch beam played across a bank of eight levers all in a lowered position. 'This is looking much more serious than I first thought.'

'Why, what's the problem?'

'Every single circuit breaker in here has been tripped. And that's never happened before in the history of Lovell, which is saying something, considering the number of electrical failures

that we've had over the years, not to mention a few direct lightning strikes.'

'So what could have caused this?'

'If there wasn't power remaining in the control room, I would
have said it might have been some sort of massive power surge
from the national grid. So maybe this is down to a rat chewing
through a critical cable, something like that.'

'How hard will it be to fix?'

'No idea – hours, days maybe. We won't know for sure until
the maintenance team has run a thorough diagnostic on Lovell.
And that means we're going to have to deal with a lot of pissed-off
post-docs and research fellows, whose projects will be bumped in
the meantime. It also means that you're not going to get to listen
to that of pulsar of yours any time soon.'

I swatted the air. 'That really doesn't matter, Steve. After all,
there will be other nights...'

Steve's gaze narrowed on me. 'As we can't do anything else
right now, do you fancy taking this experience to the next
level?'

'You have a hidden flask of coffee on you?'

'I had something even better in mind.'

'A margarita?'

He smiled, opened a metal locker, grabbed a couple of
harnesses from it and handed one to me.

'What about our shared vertigo problem?'

'I think mine is way worse than yours, and as you haven't
already vomited like I did the first time I came up here, I think
you'll more than cope with heading for the summit.'

'Seriously?'

'Yes, but once again that's another little secret for our list.
This will be my way of making the failure of this evening up to
you.'

I smiled at him. 'In that case, let's get going.'

We stepped back outside on to the gantry and made our way towards the metal staircase at the far end.

As we climbed the staircase and went up through a hatch, I braced myself. Above us, the yacht-like mast of the central receiving antenna stretching up towards the stars came into view and I found myself standing at the centre of Lovell's giant metal dish. My sense of vertigo had vanished because the curved panelling of the bowl rose around us like a stadium without any seating, meaning we could no longer see the ground far beneath us.

'Are you really ready to do this?' Steve asked, his head-torch beam flicking over the bowl as he grabbed the opportunity to inspect it.

'What else am I going to do now that you've dragged me up here?' I replied with a smile.

He grinned and clicked the carabiner from his harness on to the railing. I followed his lead.

Then the really hard part came: the final ascent towards the summit of the metal Everest.

My brief rediscovered confidence flowed away when, after a few flights of ladders, we rose above the lip of Lovell's metal bowl to reveal the landscape again. As my blood pounded in my ears, Steve started to hum 'Stairway to Heaven' again as he climbed the last ladder towards the radio telescope's focus box.

'The next time I say you need to confront your fears, just kick me,' I said.

Steve didn't reply.

Without any structure to shelter us the wind buffeted me as it tried to find gaps in my jacket. By the time we'd reached the last rung and I stepped on to a small platform around the focus box, my teeth had started to chatter.

I rested my hand on the metal container, inside which was the Multi-Beam Receiver – mounted at the exact focal point of

Lovell's bowl. It was an inspiring thought to know that all those faint radio whispers from the stars were being bounced from the metal dish back to this device.

I ignored the nagging tug of queasiness in my stomach and made myself look out at the night landscape. 'It really is spectacular up here, Steve.'

'If you say so,' he replied with a grimace as he stared straight ahead at the focus box.

'I really appreciate it.'

'No problem.' He managed a small smile as his eyes clung on to me, looking anywhere but down. 'So how about the traditional initiation selfie? You'll have to take it as I'm almost paralysed with fear.'

'No problem, although I would have refreshed my make-up back down there if you'd let me know beforehand.'

'Don't worry, you look gorgeous.'

I couldn't help myself. 'Do I?'

Steve glanced away as he took out his phone and switched on the camera, then handed it to me.

I held it up so we both filled the screen. 'Best cheesy grin please.'

Steve looked a fraction less terrified. I was feeling increasingly comfortable up here and put on my best practised selfie smile as I pressed the button and the phone's screen briefly flashed to illuminate us.

I knew it was definitely a shot for Instagram, but for a moment all I could see was a great big white rectangle burned into my vision. I blinked hard to clear my eyes, and noticed a glimmer of light dancing along the edges of each of the metal bowl's panels.

'What are you scowling at, Lauren?' Steve asked.

'Can you see some strange light covering the dish right now?'

He glanced back down briefly before his eyes snapped back

to me. 'No, but I can hear a strange noise. Maybe that's triggering your synaesthetic ability.'

'What noise?'

'Listen carefully and you'll hear it.'

I tuned in to the night-time sounds: the quiet moan of the wind, the noise of a car driving along the road in the distance... Then the faintest buzzing scratched the edge of my hearing.

'I can hear it now,' I said.

Steve nodded. 'Sounds like some sort of electrical discharge noise to me.'

'Do you think this is linked to the power spike?'

'It could be.'

The buzzing grew steadily louder until it seemed to be coming from all around us, no doubt the acoustic effect amplified by the dish. The noise was accompanied by a smell similar to burnt cinnamon.

'The last time I heard something like this was when a transformer in an old amp of mine decided to blow up,' Steve said.

'If this is linked to the power spike, then maybe we should head back to the control room to see what the readouts can tell us.'

'Good plan,' Steve replied.

We both began to descend.

Five minutes later we'd reached the floor of Lovell's bowl.

As I stepped on to the metal surface I could feel the faintest vibration through the balls of my feet. That couldn't be a good sign.

I'd begun unclipping my carabiner from the railing when a bright green spark leapt straight out from the ladder on to my exposed right hand and a teeth-grinding burning sensation swept over my skin.

'Shit!' I sucked on my fingers.

Steve stared at me. 'Are you OK, Lauren?'

'Just an electrical shock. I'll live.'

'But that shouldn't happen. This whole structure is earthed because of the threat of lightning strikes.'

'Try telling that to my fingers,' I said, flapping my hand to get rid of the tingling sensation.

Steve took his gloves off and offered them to me.

'What are those for?'

'If there's some sort of electrical fault responsible for this, you'll need to keep your hands insulated from the metalwork till we're down on the ground.'

'And what about you?'

He shrugged. 'Don't worry about me.'

I frowned at him. 'No, I don't need you to go all "knight in shining armour" on me. Give me your scarf and I'll use that to insulate myself from the structure.'

'Are you sure?'

'I insist.'

'OK...' He handed me his scarf to me.

I wrapped the heavy knitted wool round each of my hands, leaving a length between them long enough for me to still be able to manoeuvre down the ladder.

The crackling sound grew louder over our heads.

'Let's get a move on,' Steve said.

'You'll get no argument from me on that.'

We quickly descended through the hatch and ran back down the stairs to the gantry.

My gums had started to tingle by the time we'd reached the next ladder and as we began to climb down the entire metallic structure glowed with a faint green aura around us, thanks to my synaesthetic vision. And instinct told me that it wasn't a good sign.

The ten minutes of that descent felt like the longest of my

life, as I clung on to the rungs of the ladder through the slippery fabric of Steve's scarf.

The buzzing rose to a shriek as we neared the bottom of the last ladder.

'It sounds as if something really is about to blow,' I said.

'We should get clear, just in case,' Steve replied.

I leapt off the ladder a metre above the ground and Steve landed next to me. With a deafening crackle huge sparks flew out from Lovell's bowl.

'Run!' Steve shouted.

We were both racing to the control room when a blinding flare of light made our bodies cast long shadows ahead of us. We spun round to see hundred-metre-high bolts of lightning leaping from the bowl straight up into the sky with crackles of energy.

Steve placed his hands on his head. 'Holy crap, this just isn't possible.'

'I know it isn't, but it's still bloody happening.'

He nodded and we both sprinted towards the control room again.

CHAPTER THREE

WE HURTLED BACK INSIDE to be met by even more warning lights blinking on Lovell's main control panel.

Steve stared at one of the monitors. 'Bloody hell, that power spike is now sitting at over one thousand volts. No wonder we're seeing all those energy discharges from Lovell itself.'

'But where's all this power coming from?'

Steve shrugged as he squinted at the inverted lightning storm dancing out from Lovell's dish, many of the bolts earthing themselves across the Jodrell Bank site. 'This is making less and less sense by the minute.'

'So what do we do now?' I asked.

'The only thing we can do. I'm going to kill all power feeds to Lovell just in case there's a power relay stuck open, although that still wouldn't explain the number of volts we're currently registering.' He flipped up the cover on the emergency shutdown button and pressed it. The only thing that happened was a small insignificant red light joined the constellation of others on the control panel.

We both stared at the lightning storm still leaping up from the radio telescope.

Steve blew his cheeks out. 'OK, this is seriously freaking me out now.' He peered at a monitor, then clicked a button and scowled as he pushed it a few more times. 'And will you look at this? Somehow the Multi-Beam Receiver is still online and isn't responding to commands to shut it down.'

'But that's also impossible. Even if there's a short circuit somewhere, the automated systems should have kicked in.'

'Exactly. I'm open to any ideas you may have at the moment, because I have nothing.'

A totally crazy idea had occurred to me and I wrapped my arms round myself. It was so crazy I didn't want to risk voicing it. I shook my head.

'Oh, come on, Lauren, I know you well enough to see when you're holding something back.'

I sighed. 'OK, just remember that you did ask... What if Lovell is being swamped with some sort of incredibly powerful signal that's causing all these phenomena we're witnessing?'

'Including self-powering the radio telescope systems and taking over control of the Multi-Beam Receiver?'

'I'm just throwing ideas out here, Steve.'

He drummed his fingers on his lips. 'No, you're right. We should consider every possibility, however unlikely, because certainly none of the usual explanations fit.' He peered out at the lightning display. 'To start with, if this is a signal, it would have to be ridiculously strong to create what we're witnessing out there.'

'So let's check to see if this is a signal.' I grabbed the mouse and opened up the live capture window.

My mind whirled as I looked at the graphs that appeared. Hundreds of sine waves bounced up and down the screen, the data so dense there was hardly any blank space between the dancing lines.

A shiver ran through me. 'Tell me that's not a fast radio burst signal?'

'An FRB is the only thing that fits, Lauren, but the complexity of it is off the scale – not to mention its duration.'

I pointed to the strength indicator. 'But look at the power of it – two hundred and twenty-six kilowatts. This isn't exhibiting the usual characteristics of an FRB signal. It's acting more like an extreme high-frequency signal, an EHF, but even then it's at least twenty times more powerful than the strongest military hardware broadcast we've ever received.'

'You're right again. It's across an incredibly wide radio frequency too.'

I turned to Steve. 'There is one explanation we should be beginning to seriously consider.'

Steve clutched his head in his hands. 'I'm so not going there, not yet at least.'

It seemed as if neither of us were prepared to voice the idea now lurking like the proverbial elephant in the room: that this was the sort of signal SETI had been searching for years for. Could we be the first to receive a signal from an alien civilisation?

'Damn it, I need to think,' Steve said. He grabbed his yo-yo and begun pacing up and down the room while muttering to himself. He kept flicking the yo-yo to the floor and making it return to his palm with a slap.

Steve stopped pacing to say, 'Maybe, based at least on the sheer power of this broadcast, it could be coming from a source nearer to home.'

'What are you saying? That someone is deliberately sending a signal and aiming it directly at Lovell?' I asked.

'Why not? Maybe we've been caught up with some sort military test of a space-based weapon designed to jam radio systems.'

'As a woman who adores sci-fi, I would normally go for a cool tech answer. But this is so far beyond what any military force on

this planet is currently capable of that it isn't funny.' I breathed in
through my nose. 'Are we ready to leap down the rabbit hole
together yet?'

Steve shook his head. 'No, I want to rule out every other
explanation first, Lauren. You know what happened with the
team who were caught up in the famous Wow! signal.'

'Of course I do. Every astronomy student is taught how the
Ohio Big Ear telescope team thought they'd captured an extraterrestrial signal.'

'And then you also know how much rubbish they had to deal
with as well.'

'I do, but don't forget the jury is still out on what that signal
really was. And since then we've captured other FRB signals that
no one can fully explain yet.'

'That's true, but nothing on this power scale and this duration,' Steve said. 'However, there is something I'm growing
increasingly worried about. As incredible as this all is, I'm starting
to get concerned that the Multi-Beam Receiver is going to be
wrecked by what's happening.'

'But we've already tried everything to shut it down, Steve.'

'Not everything. If there is a power relay stuck open somewhere in the system, I could manually sever the power conduit to
Lovell with a fire axe and kill the power to the receiver.'

'Don't be an idiot – you could get fried to a crisp!'

'Not if I insulate myself properly.'

I crossed my arms. 'If you think I'm going to stand here and
let you go outside and get yourself killed, you've got another thing
coming, Steve.'

'And I'll never be able to forgive myself if there was something that I could have done to prevent the destruction of Lovell.
Too much blood, sweat and tears have gone into it for me to allow
that to happen.'

I knew Jodrell Bank was Steve's whole life but he was talking about Lovell as if it were something alive rather than a machine that could be fixed. Maybe I wasn't the only hopeless romantic working here.

'I can absolutely see where you're coming from, but let's do what we should have done in the first place and get Graham in to deal with this,' I said. 'After all, it's what he's paid the big bucks for.'

Steve closed his eyes. 'It may be too late by the time he gets here.'

'Look, as much as I respect you, what happens next is his call, not yours.' I took my mobile out and turned off the flight mode. I shrugged at Steve. 'Something tells me that a mobile signal isn't going to overwhelm what we're currently capturing.' I stared at the distinct lack of signal bars. 'That's strange – my phone won't connect to my network.'

Steve took out his own phone and frowned. 'Same here. It must be the strength of the signal disrupting the local cellular network.'

'Then I'll use one of the landlines.' I crossed to one of the grey plastic phones that looked like original 1970s throwbacks and started dialling.

I waited, listening to the phone ringing for a good minute before a very pissed-sounding Graham picked up at the other end.

'Who the bloody hell is ringing me at this bloody hour of the morning?' he said.

'It's Lauren from work. We need you in here now.'

'Why exactly?'

'There is no easy way to explain it over the phone, Graham. You need to get here and fast, not least to stop Steve playing the hero and putting his life on the line.'

'What the hell? Tell him not to do anything stupid till I get there.'

'Will do.' I put the receiver down and turned. 'Graham said—'

Steve had vanished.

'You damned idiot, Steve!' I shouted as I raced outside.

Lovell was at the centre of its very own glowing energy nebula as continuous lightning arced out from it like a giant version of one of those plasma ball lights that used to be popular.

I spotted Steve, who as promised had managed to find himself a fire axe and was heading straight towards Lovell with a stride that meant business.

I sprinted after him, and despite a not insignificant difference in our heights, was ready to rugby-tackle him to the ground, if that was what it took to stop the idiot. 'Graham said that you're not to do anything until he gets here!' I shouted.

Steve ignored me and carried on walking.

As I closed on him I noticed something strange about the dancing ribbons of energy. Where some of the stray lightning bolts struck the nearby buildings and treetops there was no damage whatsoever – certainly none of the secondary fires I would have expected to see from a lightning storm this intense. But that would suggest...

'Steve, stop right there! Lovell's going to be OK,' I called out.

He turned to look at me for the first time. 'What do you mean, Lauren?'

'Think the Van de Graaff generator.'

'Pardon me?'

'Watch and you'll see.' I headed straight past him, and with a prayer to the patron god of mad scientists, I closed my eyes and ran beneath the dancing ribbons of energy.

No searing pain, no final thoughts of *What the hell was I thinking?* as my brain was fried. Instead I cracked my eyes open to see I was now standing inside the cascading ribbons of energy. A whoop bubbled up from inside me and I spun around, arms outstretched as the lightning bolts streamed on to me with no more effect than if someone had been flicking me with their finger.

'Lauren, are you OK?' Steve shouted.

'Yes, absolutely fine.'

He grasped the back of his neck with his hands. 'You're either the bravest or most stupid person I've ever met in my life.'

'Takes one to know one,' I replied. 'But hopefully I've just proved to you there's no need to try to cut any power conduits.'

'So your reckless demonstration was meant to show that Lovell is basically behaving like a gigantic Van de Graaff?'

'You nailed it. When I spotted the lack of damage the lightning strikes were making, I realised there might be lots of volts but little in the way of amps. And even though this light show is beyond spectacular, based on the facts that we are still getting data from the receiver and I'm standing underneath something resembling some crazy experiment from Nikola Tesla's famous lab, we can now be certain that this EHF signal isn't doing any real damage to Lovell itself.'

Steve looked at me for the longest moment and then laughed. 'Bloody hell, I could seriously kiss you, Lauren. A brilliant bit of scientific detective work there.' He lobbed his axe away.

I grinned back at him. 'Any excuse.'

A car engine roared and a Volvo sped into the staff car park as if it were in a rally race.

Steve turned round and shook his head. 'Graham must have broken a few land speed records to get here this quickly.'

'He obviously didn't trust you not to try something stupid,' I replied.

'Look who's talking.'

Graham emerged from the car wearing a big red puffer jacket. With his glasses reflecting the lightning storm the director of astronomy ran towards us as he gawped up at Lovell. 'What the bloody hell have you done to my radio telescope? I saw this place lit up like a rave from at least five miles away.'

'I know I have my moments, Graham, but you really seriously think I could pull something like this off?' Steve replied.

'Of course not. So what the hell are we dealing with here?'

'To start with we're almost certain this is some sort of extreme high-frequency signal,' I said.

He gestured to the dish. 'An EHF signal that can do this?'

Steve shrugged. 'We're as mystified as you are. We haven't had a chance to work out the point of origin yet.'

'Then we should target the same region that Lovell is currently pointed at with the Mark II dish and run an interferometer check,' Graham said. 'Although you do realise that should have been the first thing you tried.'

'This isn't the time to have a go at Steve, Graham. Look what we're dealing with here,' I said. 'It's not exactly textbook.'

Graham peered at me and had just opened his mouth to reply when the muffled sound of a phone ringing echoed from the control room.

'That's one of the MERLIN network landlines,' Steve said.

I nodded. 'They've probably registered the data spike from Lovell over the network feed as well.'

Graham gave each of us a stern glance. 'OK, let's start putting practical plans together, but later we're going to have a serious conversation about following protocols.'

Steve rolled his eyes at me as we all rushed back into the control room.

Graham grabbed the ringing landline phone. 'Oh, hi, Richard, what can I—' The colour bled from Graham's face as he listened intently. 'OK, I'm going to put you on speakerphone so the others can hear this. Please repeat what you just told me.'

Richard's voice came over the speaker. 'We're experiencing a major phenomenon happening around the Cambridge dish.'

'Don't tell me, you've got serious low amp electrical discharges originating from your radio telescope,' I said.

'Yes, but how could you possibly know that?' Richard replied.

'Because exactly the same thing has been happening here,' Steve said. 'We've also been unable to shut Lovell's systems down.'

'Same here. Any theories on what's going on? Because we've got none – or at least none we're ready to seriously put forward.'

'We're working on it,' Graham replied.

From the sound of it, we weren't the only ones considering the ET calling Earth explanation. Reputations would be made or destroyed by how tonight played out.

Graham rested his knuckles on the desk and leant in towards the speaker. 'Richard, record all the data you can please.'

'We're on it, but it's already filled up half of our available storage.'

I crossed to one of our computers and checked the stats. 'Bloody hell, we've so far received over two thousand terabytes of data. At this rate, we're going to have to start plugging in additional storage arrays.'

Graham nodded. 'Do it. And, Richard, good luck with whatever this is.'

'You too,' Richard replied.

Graham replaced the receiver as every other phone connected to the MERLIN network started to ring simultaneously.

For the next ten minutes between us we fielded every call. The sheer extent of just how crazy this situation was became clearer by the second.

At last Steve finished the final call and shook his head. 'So that confirms it. Nearly every radio telescope across the MERLIN network around the world has been swamped with the same signal. The only notable exception being the St Petersburg telescope in Russia, who I've been unable to contact for confirmation. They aren't picking up for some reason.'

Graham nodded. 'And the strangest part is that every telescope seems to have been pointed at different regions of the sky when it happened.'

'I know I'm the least experienced here, but surely that's impossible for a radio signal? Wherever it's coming from, there has to be a common source,' I said.

'You're right of course, and that means the only logical answer is that the signal is coming from multiple targets all at once,' Steve replied.

In the distance I became aware of the faint drone of a helicopter getting louder.

I cast Graham and the others a puzzled frown. 'I thought we have clear airspace around here as otherwise it interferes with all our equipment?'

'We do unless it's an emergency,' Graham replied.

We followed him outside as the trees around the car park began to whip. A large white helicopter was coming in to land. With a roar of buffeting rotor wash, it settled on to the grass.

The moment the helicopter landed a team leapt out and started unloading silver flight crates.

A woman in a trouser suit, with short blonde hair and hard eyes, ran towards us under the still-spinning blades. When she reached us she raised an MI5 identity card displaying her photo.

The woman thrust out a hand. 'Kiera Owen, field operations director.' She gestured towards the lightning storm erupting around Lovell. 'And I'm here to help with your little problem.'

'And MI5 is involved with this because...?' I asked.

'Because Jodrell Bank is ground zero for an event that has become an issue of national security. I can't stress enough the urgency of this situation and that we need to work together so we can understand what we're dealing with before it's too late.'

Steve, Graham and I traded shocked looks as Kiera ushered us all back towards the control room.

CHAPTER FOUR

KIERA'S MEN had ferried a procession of silver crates into our control room from their helicopter. They'd already set up all manner of scientific kit from banks of oscilloscopes to a very serious-looking rack computer, which was liquid-cooled and had been built into one of the bigger crates. One of the lids had been removed to reveal ten black boxes with miniature LCD displays on each of them. One of Kiera's men, a bald-headed guy called John, their computer and encryption expert, had explained to me that it was a solid-state mass storage system that could store over a thousand terabytes. The plan was they'd use it to augment our own systems to make sure that every byte of data was successfully captured from the signal, which was showing no signs of abating anytime soon. Who knew what the other teams were doing across the rest of the MERLIN network to keep up with this huge influx of data.

Kiera gestured towards the meeting room. 'Graham, if you could gather your team in there please.'

John intercepted us as we walked past him. 'All your mobiles, please. This site is under a communications blackout until this crisis is over and that means all other forms of electronic communications, including web and email.'

'So it's a crisis now?' I asked.

'You'll be fully briefed in a moment,' Kiera said.

We started to hand over our mobiles.

'I'm not sure what good this will do. The mobile networks have already crashed around here,' Steve said.

'It's a precautionary measure.'

We followed Graham into the meeting room.

Kiera took out two official-looking documents from her briefcase. 'Steve and Lauren, you'll need to sign these copies of the Official Secrets Act.' She slid them across the table towards us.

Steve gave her a narrow-eyed look. 'And why do we need to sign these precisely?'

'So I can fully brief you about what's been going on.'

A knot of irritation tightened inside me. I'd always had a bit of an issue with authority figures. Who was she to march in here and start telling us what to do?

I crossed my arms. 'And what if we don't want to?'

Kiera's gaze tightened on me. 'Then that particular person will be escorted from this facility.'

I knew I needed to keep a lid on my annoyance, because if I didn't I would probably miss out on the biggest moment of my career. Time to toe the line, at least for now.

I took an inward breath and nodded. 'OK, OK.'

'And why aren't you asking Graham to sign one as well?' Steve asked.

Graham sat forward. 'That would be because I already have.'

Steve gave him a surprised look. 'When exactly?'

'We'll discuss that later, but first I want to hear what Kiera has to say.'

'And you will, once your team has signed their documents.' She proffered her posh pen to me across the table.

I scowled at her, took the pen and signed.

With a slight head shake Steve did the same and then rolled the pen across the desk back to Kiera.

'So what's going on?' Graham asked.

Kiera leant back in her chair. 'Thirty minutes ago, the signal you picked up with Lovell was also detected by our systems at GCHQ.'

'That's the government communications intelligence facility, isn't it?' I asked.

'Yes, and that's why this situation has rapidly escalated. You see, since receiving this signal, the GCHQ systems have been jammed across multiple radio frequencies.'

'You mean it's wiped out your ability to eavesdrop on the rest of the world's communications?' Steve asked.

It seemed I wasn't the only one with a bit of an attitude towards authority. I was starting to see Steve in a new light.

'We prefer to call it "intelligence gathering" so we can protect this country and its citizens. However, the impact of this signal doesn't stop with GCHQ's systems. You see, all transmitted communications, including satellite networks, even those with the most secure encrypted channels, are all currently offline. This signal, thanks to its sheer power, has even managed to take down our mobile phone networks. Since twenty minutes ago, the only form of viable communication has been landlines, which seem to have been spared the worst of the disruption.'

'And there was me thinking the signal was just disrupting the mobiles around here,' Steve said.

'If it were, we wouldn't be taking this as seriously as we are. Now we need answers and we need them quickly.'

Graham tapped his fingers on his chin. 'Could this all be down to some sort of solar flare activity on the scale of the Carrington Event back in 1859, which knocked out much of the telegraph network?'

'You know your history,' Kiera replied.

'I should hope so. Astronomy is my job after all.'

I managed to hold back a smile as Steve's nose twitched.

Kiera narrowed her gaze at Graham. 'A major solar flare was our first assumption too. However, the solar observatories show that there's been no significant electromagnetic activity in the sun over the last seventy-two hours, certainly nothing to warrant the scale of this phenomenon. Also, according to our final readings from GCHQ before our own systems were taken offline, Jodrell Bank seems to have been at the epicentre of this signal, which then proceeded to ripple out around the globe in a matter of seconds. It's the reason we're here. There have been huge consequences because of the effect of this signal; that's why we need to come up with a viable alternative theory.'

'A viable alternative theory to what?' I asked.

'That Russia is testing out some sort of new space-based jamming device.'

Steve gave me an *I told you so* look.

Graham shook his head. 'That sounds like raging paranoia to me.'

'I wish I could confirm that was all it was. Unfortunately, in addition to the signals, there have been other effects on our communication's infrastructure – the West's early-warning radar network that alerts us to ICBM launches has also been taken offline. We've tried reaching out to Moscow for answers, but so far nobody over there is prepared to talk to us.'

I thought of the St Petersburg team not responding to our calls and my blood chilled.

'Is this situation as dangerous as it sounds?' Graham asked, his voice almost a whisper.

'Yes, and that is why I need your help to prove it's not the Russians behind this,' Kiera replied.

Steve clenched his hands together. 'Well, there is certainly one major flaw in that theory. If it were a space-based weapon, we would be able to triangulate its position. However, we've already learnt from the other MERLIN receivers that this signal seems to be coming from all areas of the sky at the same time.'

'Yes, we realised that, but that idea has already been countered with the suggestion that Russia has somehow managed to launch hundreds of stealth satellites into low Earth orbit.'

'Oh, come on,' I said. 'How would you not know about a single one of these launches? And anyway, a satellite with a miniature nuclear reactor on board wouldn't be able to sustain the level of power we're currently seeing in this signal. Do you really think the Russians have made some sort of major breakthrough that would allow them to pull this off?'

'That's precisely the question that has got the security agencies of all the Western powers currently scratching their collective heads,' Kiera replied. 'We've certainly no previous intelligence to suggest that Russia was anywhere near developing this sort of capability. However, if they have and are happy to reveal it in such an audacious manner, it raises a more serious question.'

'Which is?' I asked.

'Is this a prelude to something much, much worse?'

Graham blinked fast and took his glasses off to wipe them on his jumper. 'Please tell me that doesn't mean what I think it does?'

Kiera gave him a thin smile. 'I wish I could, Graham. However, over the last thirty minutes, the world has been propelled towards the equivalent of a modern-day Cuban Missile Crisis.'

I let out a small gasp. 'You're not seriously saying this signal could be the prelude to all-out nuclear war?'

She gave me a straight look. 'That's exactly what I'm saying.'

It felt as if the air had emptied from the meeting room for a moment as the implications of her words sunk in.

Graham scraped his seat backwards and stood up. 'I need to ring Sarah so she can grab the kids and take them to their grandparents in—'

Kiera quickly held up her hand to silence him. 'That's not going to happen, Graham. The knowledge that I have just shared with you is obviously highly sensitive and certainly *not* to leave this facility – hence our communications blackout.'

Graham's expression darkened. 'What if I ignore you and just walk out of that door and head home anyway?'

Kiera pulled her jacket aside just enough to reveal a pistol in a shoulder holster strapped over her white shirt.

I jumped to my feet. 'You can't threaten us like this.'

'I don't want to, but I can and I will if it's the only way to get you to cooperate.' She gestured for me and Graham to sit down. 'Let's try again. I need your help, not your anger, however justified you feel it is.'

I traded glances with my colleagues. Graham looked angrier than ever but Steve's expression had become unreadable as if he were considering a chess move – a game he loved to play against the computer. I wish I knew what was going on inside that skull of his sometimes.

Graham and I sank back into our seats and slowly nodded.

'OK, that's better,' Kiera said. 'Now let's see if we can figure this out together.' She rested her elbows on the table and interlocked her fingers. 'Is there any additional information you can give me about what happened here when you first received the signal?'

'Just that we were realigning between observation targets,' Steve replied, his voice calm as if we weren't potentially staring at an end-of-world scenario. 'That's when the power first tripped out. Lauren and I went to the drive room on Lovell to manually reset the circuit breakers in there.'

'Hang on, what new target?' Graham asked. 'You were meant to stay on NGC 1277 all night.'

'That would be my fault,' I said. 'I persuaded Steve to give me some monitoring time on Lovell.'

Graham hardened his stare at Steve. 'So you decided to let your post-docs little project take priority over our scientific work?'

'It was only going to be a few minutes, Graham, and besides, we should be fostering the curiosity of our team members. At some point, we've both been in Lauren's position.'

Graham shook his head. 'That's as maybe, but it doesn't mean that this isn't a disciplinary matter—'

Kiera raised her hand to kill the conversation again. 'To stop you there, before you get too carried away with your staff issues, we have far more pressing matters to attend to.'

Graham frowned at us.

'So let me make sure I have understood this correctly,' Kiera continued. 'Lovell was realigning to this new target when you had some sort of power issue?'

'That's right,' Steve replied. 'We headed to the drive room because I thought it might be a motor glitching out. However, I couldn't reset the breaker circuits that had all tripped. Just after that we started to hear a humming sound like the noise a transformer makes but very loud.'

'So you think it was a fault with Lovell itself?'

'That's what we assumed at first, and it would certainly have explained why the power had tripped out,' Steve replied. 'However, the visual light phenomenon that Lauren witnessed suggests otherwise.'

Kiera's attention snapped to me. 'Something to do with your synaesthesia, Lauren?'

'How the hell do you know about that?' I asked.

'The first thing I did on the way over was to pull up the staff files for everyone who works here, including your own.'

So Big Brother, or in this case Big Sister, had been checking me out. I shook my head at Graham who'd raised his eyebrows at her.

Kiera opened a notebook, her pen hovering over it. 'So this audible buzzing triggered something in your visual cortex, is that right, Lauren?'

'Yes, it is.'

'And what did you see exactly?'

'A faint light running between the panels of the bowl. That was followed by static discharges. We only just made it off Lovell when the whole lightning display started up.'

'When did this occur precisely?' Kiera asked, writing everything down.

Steve's gaze flicked to his open laptop he'd brought in with him. 'According to our systems, it was 2.07 a.m. when they started to receive the signal.'

Kiera's attention narrowed on me again. 'OK, I'd like to clarify one thing, Lauren. Surely with your synaesthesia, you see visual elements like this all the time?'

'Actually, I don't. Radio telescope signals are one of the few things to trigger it, which is why I chose this particular area of astronomy for a career. But I've never seen anything like this happening on Lovell before.'

'So that suggests this audible hum has to be significant, especially if it is directly linked to the signal,' Graham said.

Steve nodded. 'OK, I may not have Lauren's gift, but I still heard it. And whoever's heard of a radio signal producing any audible sound before it's been converted? We're talking radio waves here, not sound waves.'

'So that suggests we're dealing with an entirely new

phenomenon, one possibly generated by a new class of military weapon,' Kiera said.

Steve dragged his teeth over his lip. 'It could be, but it still seems unlikely—'

The door banged open and John rushed in.

'There's been a development. I need to brief you urgently, Kiera.'

'Go ahead – everyone in here has signed on the dotted line.'

John's gaze swept over us as he nodded. 'I'm afraid the security situation has just been raised to DEFCON 3.'

Graham stared at him. 'Isn't that just a couple of steps below all-out nuclear war?'

'It is,' Kiera replied.

'How the hell could things have escalated this quickly?'

'Unfortunately it's a sign of the accelerated times we live in. You see, in the days of the Cuban Missile Crisis, they had plenty of time for a huge amount of behind-the-scenes diplomacy to avert armagedon. However, in today's interconnected world, where computers automate many of our military's responses, things can escalate far more rapidly.'

'So you're saying that some trigger-happy computers are propelling us towards a potential Armageddon?' I asked.

'Yes, and as we speak strategic bomber groups are on the tarmac warming up their engines, ready, if and when the call comes, to take to the skies. The American president will have already boarded Air Force One by now. Meanwhile, all the nuclear assets in the West's arsenal are being prepped for possible launch and the missile silo doors will be open.'

My stomach knotted so hard I thought I was about to vomit. 'Shit, this can't be happening.'

'I'm afraid it is, Lauren, and that's why I'm here. I need all your help to get to the truth of the situation, because if this isn't a

Russian attack, we need to be able to prove that to the world within the next thirty minutes – if we're going to save this planet.'

Her words struck me like hammer blows to my chest as I struggled to breathe.

Graham began to pace the room. But Steve maintained his Zen-like calm. He simply gazed across the room at Kiera and said, 'Then let's get started on saving humanity from its own stupidity and analyse this signal whilst we still have time.'

She nodded and, in a daze, I followed her and the others out of the room.

CHAPTER FIVE

IF I'D THOUGHT there had been a lot of MI5 kit in our control room before we'd left for the meeting room, it seemed to have multiplied tenfold in our absence. Now banks of additional monitoring equipment had been set up and plugged via Ethernet cables into the main control desk for Lovell.

Graham crossed to the viewing window, rested his hands on the windowsill and stared out at the on-going lightning storm.

John peered at a huge TV-size monitor that had been mounted in the middle of the room. It made our own screens look antiquated by comparison. On it, thousands of sine waves bounced up and down as they scrolled from left to right. Hundreds of red and green markers, presumably something to do with MI5's analysis of the signal, were being overlaid and updated every second.

'You've hooked up to the live data feed from Lovell then?' Steve asked.

John turned to him and nodded. 'We're streaming the data straight from your systems into our own, augmenting your data analysis tools with our own latest decrypting algorithms.'

A guy with a neatly trimmed beard nodded towards Kiera as he replaced a handset that had also been plugged into an Ethernet port back on to its cradle. 'We've just received confirmation over the secure line that Russia has raised its security level to DEFCON 2.'

'And so we edge towards the abyss,' Kiera muttered under her breath. 'OK, let Control know the moment we have a definite answer one way or the other we'll be in immediate contact.'

'Will do, ma'am.'

'Please tell me that doesn't mean the nukes are already in the air?' I asked.

Graham's back stiffened as he stared out of the window.

'No, we still have a little time to prevent that,' Kiera replied. 'However, it does mean Russia's armed forces are ready to deploy within six hours and NATO will be forced to respond in kind. But it's the next level of alert that we have to worry about, as that's critically close to the point of no return.'

The enormity of what we were dealing with began to sink in. I hadn't signed up to save the world from its own stupidity. Just knowing what I was facing meant I was fighting the urge to rush outside and vomit my few mouthfuls of pizza.

Instead I dug deeper and looked Kiera in the eye. 'But why would the Russians risk raising their alert status when they know what's at stake just as much as we do?'

Kiera shrugged. 'Because maybe this really is some sort of military weapon experiment where they are simply testing and demonstrating their technical advantage over the West to gain concessions. But if this *is* just sabre-rattling on their part, it's a hell of a risky strategy to be playing when the future of this whole planet is on the line.'

'And I wouldn't be surprised if someone in Moscow is saying precisely the same thing about the West,' Graham said, still looking out of the window.

'Then let's hope sanity prevails,' Kiera replied. 'And the best chance for that are the people in this very room, so let's get to it.'

'Just tell us what to do,' I said.

John smiled at me. 'In parallel with our own efforts, analyse the signal with the tools you have. However, you need to be aware that our initial analysis indicates that this signal contains only white noise without any sort of discernible data within it. Terabytes upon terabytes of condensed white noise, but nothing more so far. Unfortunately, without an alternative theory, this strengthens the case for this just being a jamming signal.'

'Let's not jump to conclusions,' Steve said. 'Your white noise can sound like a deep space object to us. But anyway, I may have an idea that would help prove it faster, one way or the other.'

'Which is?' Kiera asked.

'It's what scientists have always done whilst others meddle in the art of making war.'

I peered at Steve and guessed his direction. 'When the other lines of communication have been closed off between countries, scientists keep talking.'

'Precisely.'

'So tell me what you're suggesting here,' Kiera said.

'At the moment we're limited to our own experience with this phenomenon,' Steve answered. 'What we need to do is try to clarify the bigger picture and the best way to do that is to reach out.'

'You're suggesting that we talk to our colleagues in the MERLIN array at St Petersburg, aren't you?' Graham said, still not turning round.

'In one, Graham. Do that and, if they have been affected like the rest of us, it starts to show it's less likely that this is some sort of Russian attack.'

I clicked my tongue against my teeth. 'We're certainly more blind in dealing with this than we need to be. If they know anything about this phenomenon, even if it's off the record, it can only help us avert war between our countries.'

'I can see the merit in what you want to try, but I'll need to get authorisation from higher up the chain of command before I can allow you to try that,' Kiera said.

Graham spun round and glared at her. 'Oh for god's sake, Kiera. Do you really need to follow the company line at a time like this? Surely they pay you for your initiative, don't they?'

Her eyes became steel, 'I'll let the attitude slide for now because we're all under serious pressure. But for your information, there are protocols that need to be followed.'

Graham strode right up to her and thumped his fist on a cabinet. 'Protocols be damned. At any moment we could all be wiped out by the blast wave of a nuclear explosion. So forgive me for not getting out the marching band to follow you and your bloody orders!'

One of Kiera's men moved his hand to a pistol on his belt and gave her a questioning look. She shook her head slightly, and the man returned his attention to the equipment he'd been unpacking from a crate. Graham's nostrils flared bull-like at Kiera.

I'd never seen him so furious over anything. He normally resorted to hard stares rather than throw any real attitude around. But of course these were anything but normal times.

I tried reaching out for Graham's shoulder. 'Let's give Kiera a moment to get this ratified.'

He shook me off and stared at me. 'But we haven't got time for this.'

I nodded. 'I know...' I glanced at Kiera. 'Just please don't take too long.'

'I'll do everything I can to expedite the decision,' she replied.

Steve nodded, his expression still far too calm. 'Good, and in the meantime we'll start on the analysis from our end.

Maybe we can spot something that your guys have missed.' He headed over to Graham and took him by the elbow. 'I need to show you some data on my laptop from the initial signal capture.'

Graham turned to glare at him. 'All I'm fit for right now is leaping into my car and racing home to be with my family for the end. I mean, what can we do to stop this other than fiddle with our bloody computers and pretend we understand what's going on? It could take us months to unpick the truth here. And as Kiera has already bloody reminded us, time is something we haven't got a lot of.'

Steve grimaced. 'Please, Graham.'

Graham's shoulders dropped and he sighed. 'OK, OK...'

Steve grabbed his laptop. 'Lauren, you need to see this too.'

'I do?'

'Yes – I need you to study the signal phase shift analysis and give me your opinion.'

I had no idea what Steve had just said, but his eyes widened a fraction at me and I realised it hadn't been for my benefit.

'OK, you're the boss,' I replied. I followed them both out into the meeting room, a question mark growing in my mind.

Graham closed the meeting room door behind us. 'What the hell is so important about that data, Steve?'

Steve gestured towards a network point on the wall. 'That's why it's so important.' He took out a blue Ethernet cable from his jeans pocket and unrolled it.

'This isn't about that initial data capture, is it?' I asked.

'Of course not,' Steve replied. 'But just like Graham said, we don't have time to sit around on our arses waiting for Kiera to get permission for us to do the right thing. We need to reach out right now to try to get some straight answers from the St Petersburg team. Once we've done that, then maybe we can formulate a real strategy.'

'And there I was thinking you were Mr Ice, you sneaky son of a bitch,' I said.

He grinned. 'Yep, that's me.'

Graham slumped into a seat, his face looking lined. 'Who are you thinking of contacting, Steve?'

'Someone I've always considered to be a friend and who might just be able to cast some light on all of this.'

Graham nodded slowly. 'You're talking about Anton, aren't you?'

'I most certainly am.'

'Who?' I asked.

'A mutual Russian friend of ours,' Steve replied.

I stared at him. 'But if we contact him, won't Kiera hang us all for treason when she finds out?'

'If the bomb is about to drop, I don't think there'll be much time for hanging,' Steve replied.

'You reckon? Something tells me Kiera would make the time. But I agree that it's a risk worth taking.'

'Now you're thinking on my wavelength.' Steve turned to Graham. 'Can you keep Kiera distracted long enough for me to be able to do this?'

'No problem. I'll go and play the role of the obedient scientist who's realised the error of his ways.'

'Good man. You should go too, Lauren. It only needs to be one of us who faces the Wrath of Khan, and by that I mean Kiera when the shit hits the fan.'

'I'm not going anywhere, Steve.'

'You can be bloody infuriating sometimes, you know that?'

'I know, but you love me anyway, right?'

Steve rolled his eyes at me as Graham disappeared through the door and closed it behind him.

'Surely you aren't going to risk contacting this Anton guy directly?' I said. 'If it's anything like it is here, the Russian intelligence services will be crawling all over the St Petersburg facility. They'll certainly be monitoring all communications in and out in case someone on the MERLIN network tries to reach out to them.'

'And which is why I'm praying that Anton still plays online chess.'

'Huh?'

'You'll see in a moment if this goes according to plan.' With a glance towards the closed door, Steve moved his cursor towards the program menu on his laptop.

'Good luck to all of us,' I whispered under my breath as he clicked on the screen.

CHAPTER SIX

As I watched the door, the minute it took Steve to track down the old chess program felt like several lifetimes passing.

Steve shot me a triumphant look. 'Found it.'

'Get on with it then, before I pee myself with fright,' I replied. 'Although I still don't see how this is going to help.'

'This chess program comes with its own chat system, one that is so old-school that hopefully no one will think to monitor it.'

A window with a blue background appeared on the laptop screen. On it, a pixelated low-res font listed the names of available opponents. I spotted Anton's name right at the top with a green tick next to it.

I pointed to his name. 'Does that mean he's online?'

'Yes, and the swine is still number one in the rankings.' Steve clicked on a speech bubble icon next to Anton's name. A new black window containing only a flashing cursor opened up.

'That looks like Windows when it's recovering from a crash,' I said.

'I told you it was an ancient program. This thing is actually written in MS-DOS. I'm slightly shocked it even runs on this latest version of Windows.' Steve began to type in the message box, his text appearing in a lurid green glowing font:

It's about time we had that rematch, so you have the chance to regain your dignity after my crushing defeat last time.

Steve hit return.

'Is that all you're going to say?' I asked.

'Think of this as fishing and waiting for a bite. I'm hoping it should be enough to trigger Anton's curiosity.'

'OK, but surely he won't be thinking about playing a chess game if St Petersburg has been affected by this signal too?'

'If they have been, then this is exactly what Anton *will* be doing. He's something of a chess addict and it's his way to mentally relax when he needs to think things through. Like I do with my yo-yo.'

'It still sounds like a long shot to me.'

'Maybe, but if our hunch is correct and this event is playing out across the world, then Anton will almost certainly be facing a similar situation to us. And if you follow that same line of logic, he'll be trying to reach out to us too. So if the obvious lines of communication are off limits, what do you do?'

I smiled. 'You dust down an ancient chess program hoping your opposite number will be thinking the same.'

'Precisely, although the only problem is we don't know how long it might take for Anton to respond, or even if he's in a position to do so.'

I cast another nervous glance at the door and leant back in my seat. My gaze wandered across Steve's computer desktop and I noticed the minimised movie on his taskbar.

'So you've been watching the original 1950s version of *War of the Worlds* movie, Steve?'

'Of course! Absolutely the best version by far.'

A beep came from Steve's laptop and a reply appeared written in red.

Dear Steve, I'm always ready for a rematch!

Next to the message window, a chessboard in crude graphics was displayed. The white queen moved two squares up the board.

Your move, although be prepared to lose again...

Steve laughed. 'Cheeky sod.'

He typed a response. *It's been too long, dear friend.*

Tell me about it. However, I imagine the timing of you reaching out to me is more significant than simply wanting a chess game.

It is, but the first question is have you got company?

If by that you are asking if the eau de cologne favoured by Russian intelligence officers is somewhat overpowering at the moment, then you're absolutely right.

I raised my eyebrows at Steve. 'So their intelligence services are poring over their systems too.'

Steve started typing again. *But I trust the scent isn't too close at this particular moment?*

Thankfully not. I'm currently hiding in the server room, hoping they don't notice my absence for a while longer. So, we'd better be quick. I imagine you received the same incredibly powerful EHF signal that we did?

Yes, and it's currently lighting up Lovell like an out-of-control Nikola Tesla experiment.

Da! Us too.

And that's why we need to talk and quickly come up with a theory to explain what's really going on.

One simple enough for even overzealous security personnel to comprehend, hey, dear friend?

Precisely!

'So let's see if we can get to the fine detail of this with Anton,' I said. 'Ask him for the precise moment when they first received the broadcast.'

Steve nodded and began typing. *What time did you first receive the signal?*

At 02.08 GMT.

'Ours was earlier – at 02.07 GMT,' I said. 'As far as we know, we were the first to receive it.'

'Then let's see if we can confirm a few other details,' Steve said.

What was the power of the signal?

In excess of 200 gigahertz. Incredibly the signal appears to be powering our systems despite the mains feed being cut to it.

Exactly the same is happening here. Although it appears Lovell was the first dish to capture the signal at 02.07 GMT before spreading out around the globe.

And are your authorities acting as paranoid as ours are? Anton asked.

Steve paused and gazed at me. 'How much should I tell him?'

'Everything, Steve. If he doesn't know already, he needs to. He might be in a position to convince others, just like we hope to.'

He nodded. 'An academic pincer movement might help, although this does feel as if we're about to cross some sort of line.'

'I think we crossed that line some time ago,' I replied, then moved to the door and wedged a chair up beneath the handle.

Steve started typing again. *Anton, I'm not sure if you know this, but the West believes this is some sort of Russian attack and a prelude for a full nuclear strike.*

Oh my god. I was hoping that your authorities would be somewhat less paranoid than ours.

No such luck, my friend, Steve typed. *The question is, have you any ideas about how we can stop them leaping over the edge and dragging the whole world with them?*

Now that we can confirm both the systems in your country and the West have been affected, it must make a difference, surely?

My problem will be convincing them that this is the truth, Steve replied.

Da. Although we're both taking huge risks, the alternative is far, far worse. I will do everything I can to cool the hotheads over here.

And we'll do the same, my friend, Steve typed.

The door banged hard against the chair.

'Open this bloody door before I kick it down!' Kiera shouted from the other side.

'Let's just hope you're wrong about the Wrath of Khan, Lauren,' Steve said.

'If not, I just want you to know that working with you has been the happiest time of my life.'

He threw me a small smile. 'Always good to hear.'

I crossed to the door, took a breath and pulled the chair out.

The door flew open at once and Kiera barged in, her pistol already aimed across the meeting-room table – directly at Steve. 'Close that bloody laptop now! My team has just detected an unauthorised communication from this room. What the hell have you done, Steve?'

He shut the laptop and raised his hands. 'I just took the initiative and reached out to someone,' he replied, his voice calm.

Kiera glowered at him, leant across the meeting-room table and grabbed the laptop, yanking its Ethernet cable from the wall. 'Just give me one good reason why I shouldn't shoot you right now for being a traitor?'

My heart banged in my chest. I could read the fury in Kiera's eyes and feared that she might actually shoot him. With cold sweat soaking my armpits, I stepped into her path and pulled the muzzle of her gun to my chest.

'If you are going to shoot Steve, then you can shoot me as well because I helped him do this,' I said.

'Lauren, this is between me and Kiera,' Steve said.

'Wrong, it's between all of us. Reaching out to the St Petersburg facility was always going to be the most sensible play.'

'You did what?' Kiera said. Her eyes became slits and her finger started to tighten on the trigger.

I breathed the slightly musty smell of the room and closed my eyes, bracing myself for a bullet to pierce my chest.

'Why the hell are you aiming a weapon at one of my staff?' Graham's voice shouted.

I opened my eyes and looked past Kiera to see Graham in the doorway behind her.

'I'm about to shoot these two for betraying their country.'

'Will you bloody listen before going all *Die Hard* on us?' I said. 'Because of his bravery, Steve may have actually saved this whole stupid world of ours!'

Kiera squeezed her eyes shut, breathed out slowly and lowered her weapon a fraction. 'You have precisely thirty seconds to convince me.'

Steve stood up. 'I just spoke to my opposite number who runs the MERLIN radio telescope facility in St Petersburg.'

The tip of Kiera's thumb tapped the stock of her gun. 'I told you I was trying to get clearance for you to do exactly that.'

'With all due respect each second counts and what Steve found out changes everything,' I said.

Kiera gave Steve a weary look. 'Go on then...'

'It turns out that the St Petersburg radio telescope is being swamped right now too. If this is some sort of cyberattack designed to neutralise early-warning systems, it isn't just the West that's been affected.'

'And you seriously expect me to believe that? What's to say that your contact didn't have a gun being held to his head as he spoke to you?'

Steve stared at her and then his shoulders fell. 'Yes, that's a possibility, but I've known him my entire professional career.'

Something that looked almost like sympathy crossed Kiera's face for a moment. 'It's also a classic counter-intelligence technique. Wrap truth round a lie to help reinforce what we want to hear during a time like this.'

I stared at Steve. His face had become ashen. Had Anton been compromised? Was that it? But every instinct told me otherwise.

'No, I'm sorry, but that doesn't make any sense,' I said.

'Why not?' Graham said. 'As much as I admit it, Kiera does have a point.'

'Because her version supports what amounts to a zero-sum game,' I replied.

Kiera tilted her head to one side. 'What do you mean?'

'Regardless of who pulls the trigger first, nobody wins the prize in an all-out nuclear exchange. Everyone knows that.'

Graham nodded. 'And the Russians have just as much to lose as we have.'

'Which means the only logical explanation is that this phenomenon has nothing to do with Russia or the West,' I said.

'To me that still sounds as if you're relying on hunches and prayers,' Kiera replied.

'And you're also basing decisions on a bigger assumption that the Russians would be stupid enough to telegraph their intentions by taking out the West's early-warning systems,' I said. 'That doesn't sound like much of a military strategy to me.'

Kiera was about to respond when John pushed past Graham into the room.

'There's been another major development, Kiera,' John said. He glanced at the gun in her hand. 'And one that is probably relevant to the situation in here. The signal has stopped dead and that's not all – it's ceased across all our monitoring stations simultaneously, according to the communiqué from London we've just received. All our early-warning radar systems are back online and there is no sign of any enemy activity. The threat level has been reduced to DEFCON 4.'

'You mean it's over?' I replied.

'Nuclear war seems to be off the table for the moment,' John replied.

We exchanged stunned glances and then Steve whooped. I threw my arms around him as he spun me around.

'Oh thank god!' Graham said.

John held up his hand. 'However, we do have a new problem. The huge amounts of data that have been captured at the other receiving sites is now being downloaded on to the computers at this facility, and certainly not by us. We thought it was random data at first, but initial analysis indicates it's actually code that's been exposed to some sort of sophisticated fractal compression. It's expanding and seems to be compiling itself into a single program at this facility.'

Graham nodded slowly. 'Of course, data can appear like white noise unless you have the right key.'

'A key that has somehow turned this program on within our own systems,' I said.

'But what sort of program are we talking about here, John?' Kiera asked.

'We have no idea yet – it's still compiling. However, Control have ordered us to begin Operation Digital Fortress to contain it before it finishes its compile.'

Kiera gave him a grim look. 'Then do it.'

She strode out of the room after John and the three of us exchanged long glances.

'Looks as if our execution is on hold – for now, at least,' Steve finally said.

I turned to Graham. 'And you might need to start dusting down this planet's first contact protocols.'

Graham gave me an unreadable look that was anything other than surprised.

But Steve was gawping at me. 'Seriously, Lauren?'

'I think we have just eliminated every other possibility,' I said with fresh excitement churning inside me.

CHAPTER SEVEN

WE ENTERED the control room to see Kiera and her team gathered around the large monitor watching a series of ones and zeros scrolling across the screen.

'Is that binary code?' Steve asked as we joined the group.

'It appears to be,' John replied. 'But the really puzzling thing is, if it's alien in origin, how can it be compatible with our own computer systems?'

'So we're really going there that this is from aliens?'

'There was always a possibility it was an extraterrestrial signal,' Kiera replied.

'So why let the world be dragged to the edge of Armageddon if you thought there was a chance it wasn't the Russians?' I asked.

'That had to be our default response in case it really was the opening move for a pre-emptive strike,' Kiera replied. 'Any hesitation on our part to take that threat seriously would have left us exposed in a worst-case scenario.'

'We can talk about the rights and wrongs of that later,' I replied. 'However, why are you now seriously thinking this could be a first contact situation, especially when the power of the signal would suggest it's coming from a local source?'

'Because we've already received a signal sporting some of the same characteristics,' Kiera replied. 'Isn't that right, Graham?'

Steve whirled round to face him. 'What's she talking about?'

Graham's shoulders fell. 'Can I brief them, Kiera?'

'You can go ahead now that they've signed the Official Secrets Act.'

He gave us both a long look. 'Six years ago, here at Jodrell Bank, we received a signal that our analysts believe may have been alien in origin, even though it appeared to come from a nearby source.'

I found myself gawping at him.

Steve was the first to find his voice. 'If that's true, why have we never heard anything about it, let alone the rest of the world?'

'Let's just say that a huge amount of pressure was applied to everyone who worked at the facility at that time to make sure it was never leaked,' Graham replied, casting a razor-eyed look towards Kiera.

Steve growled. 'God give me strength, Graham. It might have bloody helped tonight if you had started off by telling us that there was a signal before this one.'

'That wasn't my call.'

'Graham's right, because it was mine, and we're telling you now,' Kiera said.

'So that's why you'd already signed the Official Secrets Act,' I realised.

Graham nodded.

Steve looked between Graham and Kiera, clenching his fists so hard that his knuckles turned white.

I stepped in front of him in case he did something epically stupid. 'OK, we can play the blame game later, but we have more urgent matters to deal with. Graham, was the original broadcast like this one?'

Graham glanced at Kiera.

'Tell them everything,' she said.

'No, it was nothing like as powerful, and it certainly didn't actively take over systems like this latest signal seems able to. It was also different in another key way. It was a distress signal transmitted in English and it contained a looped voice recording.'

My skin tingled. 'What did it say?'

'It was from a pilot called Angelique calling for assistance. According to the message, her ship, *Athena*, had been left drifting after some sort of battle.'

For a moment my mind scrabbled to process what Graham had just said.

Steve stared at his best friend and shook his head. 'All these years you've held this from me. I really can't believe you.'

Graham's gaze skated away from Steve's.

'But when you say "ship"...?' I asked.

Graham spread his hands wide. 'A spaceship, a boat at sea, who knows? The one thing we can be certain of was that this signal didn't originate from our world.'

Steve clenched his fists even harder. 'So you're telling us that we have had a bona fide first contact situation and the government has clamped down on that information ever since?'

Graham couldn't meet Steve's eyes. 'Yes...'

Steve grabbed his yo-yo and started pacing up and down. 'You bloody people.'

'Your friend just did what he was told to do,' Kiera said. 'But as Lauren attempted to do a moment ago we need to move this conversation on. And to do this you have to understand the context. This latest signal has just been the most recent event in a series of contacts with alien species.'

My question came out as a whisper. 'Species as in plural?'

Even Graham was looking surprised.

'Yes, there have been multiple contacts, from UFO intercepts to direct interaction with non-terrestrial creatures,' Kiera replied.

'You mean that disbanded Pentagon UFO unit that released the video of F18 pilots chasing a weird spinning craft wasn't just pursuing some top-secret military vehicle?' I asked.

'No, it was the real deal and just one of many encounters. Some of them have been far more extreme.'

Steve's expression twisted. 'So you're telling us the UFO conspiracists have had it right all this time?'

'Not all of them, but a few came very close to the truth. However, this latest signal, along with the original voice recording, doesn't fall into the same category as the other encounters.'

Maybe I was dreaming all of this. Maybe I'd fallen asleep binging Netflix at home. I tried to keep my voice steady. 'And that's because?'

'When our experts analysed the original voice signal through a process of triangulation with other receivers around the world, the signal appeared to originate at an altitude of two thousand feet over a small town in Oklahoma,' Kiera replied. 'However, when the US scrambled military jets to intercept the signal whilst it was still broadcasting, nothing was found at the coordinates.'

'Could it have been a craft with a type of very advanced stealth technology?' I asked.

'Even if it was, we would have detected something. Previous verified UFO encounters have been picked up by our radar systems.'

Steve shook his head slowly. 'God, you lot and your ability to suppress the truth. Conspiracies layered beneath conspiracies, oh what a surprise.'

I rested my hand on his shoulder. 'We need to take a deep breath here, Steve.'

His eyes caught mine. 'I know, I know.'

I turned my attention to John. 'Do you have any theories about how alien code can possibly run on a human-designed computer?'

'From what I've seen so far it seems to have actively altered its code into a binary format to make it compatible.'

Steve's expression sharpened. 'That's seriously impressive, isn't it?'

'Very. Certainly nothing that we have ever produced could hope to match what this code has already achieved across multiple non-compatible systems with the level of control that a human hacker could only fantasise about.'

I put my hands on my head. 'I can't believe we're seriously having this conversation about an alien program.'

Steve nodded. 'Me too.' He glanced at Graham. 'Everything I thought I knew is being turned upside down.'

Graham met Steve's eyes for the first time since this conversation had started. 'That's how I felt too, Steve, and I wish I could have told you before, but I couldn't. And I also realise how difficult this must be for you and Lauren to take on board, but based on my own experience of living with this secret for the last six years it will rapidly become your new reality. And with that level of shift in your world view nothing will be the same for either of you ever again.'

To live with that sort of secret all that time... 'I can far too easily imagine what that must have been like for you, especially not being allowed to discuss something so incredible with anyone else,' I said.

Graham nodded. 'It certainly hasn't been easy.'

Steve actually gave his friend a small smile and the tension in the room notched down a fraction. 'I can imagine.'

'I'm really sorry, my friend,' Graham replied.

'I know you are,' Steve replied.

'At least this time you don't have to bear this burden alone,' I said.

'That's very true, so let's see if we can get to the bottom of what's going on now,' Graham replied.

Steve turned to John. 'OK, if this latest signal wasn't from this world, but didn't come from a single source, what explanation have you guys come up with for that? You must have one, right?'

'There is an extreme possibility that it was the original signal and that particular transmission actually came from a parallel version of Earth,' John replied.

I gave him a long hard stare. 'So along with everything else, you're now trying to tell us that your people believe you have evidence that multiverses exist?'

'It's actually been a hypothesis for quite some time to explain where at least some of the UFO craft originate from.'

Steve gave him a slow clap. 'This night just gets better and better. I'll need to hang out on conspiracy websites and post some updates after this. Those guys are going to love all this.'

Kiera scowled at him. 'Please don't make me regret my decision to fully brief you.'

I crossed my arms. 'Will you stop with all the implied threats already, Kiera? You've just dropped the biggest revelation in history on us, so don't be surprised if we need a moment to adjust to it.'

'Sorry if you misunderstood me. It wasn't an implied threat; it's a very real and implicit one,' Kiera replied.

Steve shook his head. 'Graham, I'm starting to get an insight into what you had to deal with after the original signal.'

'Exactly that, I'm afraid. And take my word for it, these guys are experts at finding your pressure points.'

I shook my head at Kiera and returned my attention to John. He seemed far more reasonable to deal with than his officious boss. 'Are you certain that this latest signal is from a nearby parallel world source?'

'We won't know until we've had more time to analyse it,' he replied.

Graham raised an eyebrow. 'Actually there is a very quick way for us to work out if this signal has travelled millions of light years to reach us or not.'

I nodded. 'We should have thought of this earlier.'

John gave us a puzzled frown. 'Why, what are you suggesting?'

'It's easier if we demonstrate,' Graham said. He crossed to one of our computers and pulled out the data capture roster for tonight's session. He clicked on the attached file and turned on the computer's speaker to press play.

At once the sound of static filled the room and my vision started to dance with spots of light.

'That's the sound of this signal?' Kiera asked.

Steve nodded. 'And I realise it sounds like random white noise to you, but that's because the signal is so complex. The difficulty comes in trying to work out if it actually contains anything but random noise. We now know, in this case, that it contains sophisticated code.'

The blurred points of light began to focus in my eyes...

'Apart from the small clue it swamped your systems and is now compiling itself into some sort of program,' John said.

Steve snorted. 'That aside.'

The spots of light converged and formed a series of geometrical symbols that superimposed themselves over my view of the control room. 'Guys, I'm guessing none of you are seeing anything odd at the moment?'

Everyone looked at me and shook their heads.

'That's what I thought. It appears that as I'm listening to the signal, it's triggering something very specific with my synaesthesia and I can tell it's not random.'

Kiera stared at me. 'Why, what are you seeing, Lauren?'

'A sequence of circles, squares and triangles all pulsing rapidly in front of me.'

'But how can the signal be triggering your ability so specifically like this?' Steve asked.

'A great question – I've only ever seen random patterns before. This is almost as if the signal has been written in a way that can utilise my synaesthesia as a means to communicate.'

'How can that even be remotely possible?' Kiera asked.

I shrugged. 'Maybe its creators have a form of synaesthesia themselves and they constructed a language around it.'

'OK, that's certainly worth considering,' Kiera said.

'Lauren, if you're right, with your ability we could have the key to deciphering this, if it is a language,' John said.

A pulse of excitement ran through me. 'I'm certainly up for that.'

Graham looked at Steve and then me. 'And have you both noticed the other significant detail about the sound of the signal?'

My eyes widened as I realised what he meant. 'There's no whistling noise in the background.'

'You're absolutely right,' Steve said, beaming at us.

'And the significance of this is?' Kiera asked.

'If a radio signal is coming from a source such as a pulsar on the other side of the universe, by the time a dish like Lovell captures it, it's already passed through millions of light years of space in between,' Graham replied. 'During that journey, the radio signal would have to pass through gas nebular, hit tiny particulates of matter – general navigation through the detritus of deep space. And as it hits all those little speed bumps, they cause a radio signal to deviate slightly. It's that deviation, however small, that creates the background whistle that grows exponentially the further away from Earth the signal's source is.'

'And with this signal, there's no whistle, so that confirms it was created by a closer source?' Kiera asked.

'That's what this quick kick-the-tyres test would suggest,' I replied.

John scratched his neck. 'So it sounds as if we're already narrowing this down to being another broadcast from a parallel world. However, unlike the original signal, this time the signal seems to have come from multiple sources.'

Instinctively I could feel we were on the right track now and a tingle of excitement was growing in my stomach. 'So then we come back to what this program was designed to do?'

A chime came from the MI5 computer system.

'I think we're about to find out,' John replied.

The monitor glitched in front of us.

My skin prickled as a single word appeared:

Sentinel.

Steve whooped and punched the air. 'It looks as if we've just received another message from a parallel world.'

CHAPTER EIGHT

COULD we have really just received a message from a parallel dimension? A tingling sensation ran through me as the enormity of this began to sink in.

So the human race wasn't alone in the cosmos and we'd just been handed direct evidence of it, even if the *aliens* were next door in another parallel Earth. And somehow, impossibly, they were able to use my synaesthesia to communicate with us.

Right person, right time, right place, a coincidence – or could Lovell had been targeted *because* someone with synaesthetic ability worked there? My mind tilted on the edge of a precipice as I glanced to the window, half expecting to see an alien peering at me and nodding. No, that just had to be luck. After all, at least one in two thousand people had synaesthesia. Not that many, but not crazy odds either.

I returned my attention to the signal.

Around us the sound of the static began to rise and fall like the crashing of storm waves upon a shore. The symbols flowing across my vision intensified and every screen in the control room glitched briefly before the same word appeared on each and every one.

Sentinel.

'How can this be happening, John? I thought you'd locked the code down in our computer using Digital Fortress protocols?' Kiera asked.

'It shouldn't be able to do this, but based on the fact that the code has cut straight through our firewalls like a blowtorch through tinfoil, we may be dealing with some sort of sophisticated computer virus.'

'Whatever happened to the *we come in peace* speech?' Graham said, shaking his head.

'In that case, initiate phase two of Digital Fortress immediately,' Kiera said.

John rushed to the network rack and ripped out the Ethernet cables tethering it to our wall sockets. He wiped a bead of sweat from his forehead. 'All physical connections to the outside world have been severed. The virus is now effectively sandboxed on our system. However, to be on the safe side, I would recommend that until further notice we also cut all contact on MI5 operative mobile communications and with the outside world too, to make sure that we leave no avenues open for this virus to escape this facility.'

Kiera nodded and clapped her hands together. 'OK, everyone, please hand all your phones over to John until further notice.'

John started walking around the room, gathering up the team's phones.

'Can you be sure this thing is really a virus, Kiera?' I asked.

'We can't take the risk that it isn't and it's always safer to assume the worst case,' she replied. 'If there is hostile intent here, at least they won't catch us on the back foot.'

I could understand her caution and could even see the sense

in it, but I instinctively felt it was the wrong way to handle this situation.

John approached Kiera with a bulging bag of phones. I assumed mine was in there too.

'I'll need your mobile, Kiera,' he said.

'Of course.' She handed it over to him.

John closed the bag. 'I'll just go outside and grab the phones of our two guys guarding the perimeter.'

Kiera gave him a distracted nod as she gazed intently at me. 'Are you still seeing those symbols, Lauren?'

'Yes, and sharper than ever,' I replied.

'Then we need to explore your theory that they're some form of language. For all we know the program may have already given us the *we come in peace* speech, and we just haven't been able to understand it yet.'

'Worryingly you're almost starting to sound reasonable now,' Steve said.

'Aren't I full of surprises?' Kiera flashed him the briefest smile but then her normal hard, thin-lipped expression returned. 'Lauren, maybe the first step is for you to transcribe what you're seeing and for us to send it off to our cryptologists to decode after John's had a look.'

'That makes sense,' I replied.

I settled myself into a chair and picked up a pad as the shapes continued to dance within my vision. Next to me, I noticed a green light blinking on the webcam clipped to the top of the computer station. In a corner of the large screen a video window showing real-time footage of me appeared.

John appeared in the doorway of the control room and stared across at the video images of me that were now on every screen in here.

'I thought you cut the connection to the outside world, John?' Kiera said.

'I did,' he replied.

Steve gestured to the webcam. 'Are you sure? Because it looks as if someone is trying to start a video chat session with Lauren right now.'

'Could it be Anton from St Petersburg?' I asked.

John glanced at the network rack and shook his head. 'As I said, every external connection has been cut. Maybe it's an internal source somewhere on this facility?'

Kiera's gaze sharpened on Graham. 'You have told us about all your staff on site, haven't you?'

'Of course I have,' he replied, as he shot Steve a questioning look.

Steve held up his hands. 'I promise we're the only ones who have been on site tonight.'

My own huge image on the big screen stared back at me. 'This couldn't be the alien program doing this, could it?'

John scratched his ear. 'Possibly, but why?'

Steve's eyes widened. 'What if it's another attempt to communicate with us?'

'How exactly?' Kiera asked.

'Try talking to the webcam, Lauren,' Steve said.

My mouth grew dry as I peered at the webcam. 'Why are you here?'

The video of me suddenly looped and white dots appeared over my face, marking out the movement of my lips and eyes.

John peered at it. 'That looks like some form of facial-scanning algorithm—'

An ear-piercing shriek cried out from the speakers, cutting John off and filling the control room. We all clamped our hands over our ears, but as quickly as the sound had roared up it began to soften again to a more comfortable level.

I gazed with a sense of fresh wonder as a green colour started to bleed into the symbols floating before my eyes. Of all the things that I might have expected to enter my mind, it wasn't an old memory that I hadn't thought of in years...

It had been in the middle of the night, when an old school friend I'd lost contact with had called me from Australia having tracked me down via a mutual friend on Facebook. As she'd told me about how she'd moved to Melbourne with her boyfriend to work as a graphic designer, I'd been filled with a sense of intense happiness at being reunited with my long-lost friend. The feeling was so powerful it was as if I was reliving it now. Then the static ebbed to silence, the memory faded and the symbols disappeared with it. At once the feeling of happiness vanished from within me.

'Whoa!' I said.

'Did the program just respond to you asking it a direct question?' Kiera asked as she rubbed her ears.

'I think so, but not in the way you might think. Just let me try something to confirm it.' I returned my attention to the webcam. 'What's your purpose here?'

Once again, there was a shriek of intense noise, but slightly quieter than last time. The symbols appeared, but this time they were tinted red and a fresh memory flooded through me...

I'd been in Birmingham, walking back from a pub late one night when a guy had started to follow me. Every instinct had told me I was in danger. I'd almost run into an Indian restaurant for safety, but just then the guy had walked on. I'd called a taxi home anyway. At first, I thought I'd just been paranoid, until the next day I'd seen on the news that a similar-looking guy had attacked a woman that same night. I'd then suffered a major guilt trip about not immediately ringing the police to report him.

My heart raced and my palms grew sweaty as the same feeling of dread that I'd experienced that night returned to me.

I swivelled in my seat to face the others. 'I have no idea how, but the symbols that I'm seeing are also triggering specific memories with very strong emotions attached to them. When I asked why Sentinel was here, it triggered a memory of a reunion with a friend. However, when I asked what his purpose was, a memory of a moment when I'd been in danger surfaced.'

Kiera's face tensed. 'So this Sentinel program is here because there is some sort of threat to us? Or is he the threat?'

'Lauren, why don't you ask the program directly?' John said, his eyes sliding towards the door.

I nodded and returned my attention to the webcam. 'Are you the threat to us?'

The symbols shifted back to green in my synaesthetic vision and once again the memory of my old friend surfaced.

I turned to the others. 'I'm as certain as I can be that this code isn't the threat here.'

'Can you try asking who or what the threat is?' Steve said.

I peered into the lens. 'Can you explain what the threat to us is?' I asked.

The symbols turned purple and a complex formula appeared, hovering before my eyes.

'Quick, give me a pen,' I said.

John handed me an expensive-looking rollerball pen and I started to scribble down a formula. I was certain I recognised it from university.

Graham peered at it. 'That looks like part of an equation for dark energy.'

'I knew it looked familiar,' I replied. I peered again at the camera. 'Is the threat something to do with dark energy?'

The formula vanished from my vision and was replaced by yellow symbols. A new memory began to surface...

I'd been sitting in a coffee shop when I'd hit send on my job application to work at Jodrell Bank, a decision that I'd known was utterly right for me. And once again that was what I was feeling now: certainty.

'Yes – I've just had another memory that seems to confirm it's something to do with dark energy.'

'Interesting,' John said to himself.

'We should really plan a list of questions so we can do this in a structured way,' Graham said.

Kiera nodded. 'I agree. Lauren, it seems as though you have become our unofficial translator. Would you like to make that more official and continue with us as a consultant after tonight?'

'I'd be happy to   at least if they can spare me from this place for a while.'

Steve sighed. 'Do you know how hard it is to find a good post-doc person? And you are one of the best, Lauren.'

'But we won't stand in her way either, will we, Steve?' Graham said.

He slowly shook his head. 'Of course we won't. Anyway, I could be wrong here, but based on the way the code is communicating and responding directly to Lauren's questions, I think this could be some sort of true artificial intelligence. Could that be right, John?'

John drew his gaze back from the control-room window he'd been staring out of. 'Going by everything we've seen so far, it's certainly a strong possibility.'

'So now we're saying this is an alien AI from a parallel dimension?' Graham asked.

'Why not?' Steve said. 'After all, it's a rather neat way for an alien race to send an ambassador to another world, even another dimension, and all at the speed of light of the signal. It also deals with the problem of trying to beam back a reply to god knows where, when you can ask their AI representative the question directly.'

Graham whistled. 'An AI venturing between parallel worlds, now that really is an astounding thought.'

'I've seen things you people wouldn't believe,' Steve said.

'Pardon?' Kiera said.

But I knew exactly what Steve was saying and it was actually a film quote. 'It's a speech by the replicant Batty from *Blade Runner*.'

Kiera shook her head. 'Right, and your point being, Steve?'

'That we need to start thinking of this code as something alive.'

'I agree,' I said. 'And if so we should give it a name.'

'Well, the only English word we've seen so far is Sentinel, so let's run with that,' Steve said.

Kiera shrugged. 'Can we really be sure that this is an AI and not a virus?'

'We can ask Sentinel a direct question to find out,' I said. I focused on the webcam. 'Sentinel, what are you exactly?'

Pink symbols appeared and another memory flooded through me...

I'd climbed Mount Fuji to watch the sun rise. I'd never felt so utterly alive in my life as I had at that moment as the first rays of the sun had bathed my face.

I laughed. 'Yes, it seems that Sentinel is very much alive.'

'This is seriously epic,' Steve said.

Kiera nodded. 'OK, now we know we have a dialogue with this Sentinel AI, we need to ask him about his reference to dark energy and whether it's something to do with the danger he mentioned.'

I nodded. 'So get me some fresh coffee and—' The words died on my lips as red symbols appeared in my vision and a feeling of deep dread flooded me.

'Lauren?' Steve asked.

A bitter taste tanged the back of my mouth. 'I—'

I stopped as a bright ball of light blossomed outside and bathed the room with orange. A split second later a deep rumble shook the walls and the control-room window cracked. In the distance the staccato beat of automatic gunfire started up, interspersed with single shots.

We rushed over to the crazed windows to stare out at dark plumes of smoke and flames rising from the helicopter into the night sky. Two of Kiera's men were hunkered down behind a couple of cars, returning shots with shadowy figures lurking in the treeline further out, lit up by the flashes of their own weapon fire.

Kiera whirled round. 'We're under attack. We need to protect the—'

She was cut off as impossibly loud gunshots resounded around us. The two MI5 officers who'd remained at their terminals suddenly slumped on to their keyboards.

Disbelief and shock slammed into my mind as Kiera's hand darted towards her own holster.

'I wouldn't do that if I were you, Kiera,' John said, pointing his gun at her. 'Your weapon please.'

I stared at him, hands clenched. 'What are you doing, John?'

'What I'm paid to do,' he replied, his voice iron. 'And in a moment I'm going to walk out of here with the computer containing Sentinel's code, and with you, Lauren, coming with me to assist us, and the rest of you aren't going to do *anything* to stop me.' He gestured with his hand again and, with a scowl, Kiera handed her weapon over that he stashed in his belt.

I exchanged shocked glances with Steve and Graham. This couldn't be happening.

'I don't know what you've got yourself into, but if you do this there's no going back, John,' Kiera said.

He gestured towards the dead bodies of the other agents. 'That's a bit of a moot point now, Kiera. Besides, there was no going back from the moment I was first inserted into MI5 as a sleeper agent.'

Kiera gasped and then slowly shook her head. 'Who the hell are you working for? You owe me that at least.'

'I owe you nothing.'

'But you know you'll be hunted down for the rest of your life.'

John laughed. 'You still have no idea about what you're dealing with here. Besides, it's your own immediate future, Kiera, and those of the other civilians in this room, that I would be more concerned about if I were you. If anyone moves so much as a millimetre to help Lauren or to stop me, I warn you now, you will be executed.' He gestured towards us with his gun up and everyone raised their hands, including me as my heart threatened to rip its way out of my chest.

CHAPTER NINE

GUNFIRE CONTINUED to crackle outside as John strode towards the crated rack computer that contained Sentinel's code.

Something inside me hardened and, before my brain had a chance to stop me, I found myself standing between John and the MI5 computer, my hands planted on my hips. 'You can't do this, John.'

He raised his gun towards me. 'You need to start thinking like a hostage, because that's exactly what you are.'

I crossed my arms. 'This is the second time today that someone has threatened me with a weapon. It didn't impress me then and it doesn't impress me now.'

Kiera, her arms still raised, gave me the slightest headshake, but I ignored her.

'I'm not messing around here, Lauren,' John said. 'Shift your arse now or pay the consequences.'

I did my best to keep the tremor out of my voice as I said, 'That's a shame, because I'm not going anywhere.' My gamble, my crazy stupid gamble, was that John was actually a decent guy at heart who could still be reasoned with.

'Don't be an idiot, Lauren – this isn't worth throwing your life away for,' Steve said from behind me.

John raised his eyebrows. 'Listen to your boyfriend if I were you.'

'He's not my...' I flapped my hand at him. 'Oh, whatever.'

'I haven't got time for your pointless heroics.'

'Just give me one good reason why you'd do something like this and then maybe I'll play along.'

The lines smoothed around John's eyes. 'This is all part of a much bigger plan to keep this world safe.'

'Safe from what exactly?' Steve asked.

'Let's just say this latest incident with Sentinel is just the tip of a very substantial threat to the world – a threat that we've been dealing with since the last century.'

'You mean other previous alien encounters, don't you?' I said.

'Yes, I do,' John replied. 'Our world has been under threat for years now – from enemies far more technologically advanced than our own.'

'So you're saying these aliens are hostile?'

'Very much so, which is why we're not going to take chances with this Sentinel AI, and we're certainly not prepared for it to fall into the hands of this or any other governments.' John waved the tip of his gun sideways. 'Lauren, now please get out of my way before you make me do something I regret.'

I gestured with my head towards the two dead agents. 'That didn't seem to stop you when you murdered your colleagues just now.'

'They were MI5 operatives who knew the risks of their career. You're a civilian.'

I crossed my arms. 'Still not moving.'

'I'm sorry, but you can't say I didn't warn you.'

I stared defiantly back at him. Surely he wouldn't? 'But you need me to translate.'

John's eyes became ice-cold. 'Your synaesthesia isn't a unique ability. You can be replaced if necessary.'

But then Steve was by my side, his arms crossed too, as if we were posing for our indie band photo.

'If you're going to shoot Lauren, you're going to have to kill me too,' he said.

I stared at Steve. 'Seriously?'

'Look, I'm doing my best here to convince you that I'm a decent guy and maybe even boyfriend material.'

Despite everything, I couldn't help smiling. 'You totally wonderful idiot.'

'Enough already,' John said. He aimed his gun at Steve and his finger started to squeeze the trigger.

It felt as if an ocean's worth of adrenalin flooded my body in that microsecond.

I launched myself at John and knocked his gun hand upwards. A flash of light blazed from his pistol's muzzle and, with a bang, a bullet punched a perfectly circular hole in the ceiling. Better there than Steve's chest at least.

But John's MI5 training had already kicked in and he chopped hard into the side of my neck with his other hand.

Numbing pain burst through me and I crumpled to the ground. I caught a blur of movement from the corner of my eye.

Kiera darted forward and scissor-kicked John in the chest. He hurtled backwards over a desk and she was on top of him instantly, grappling with him for his gun.

John twisted and struck out across her face. But Kiera hung on and together they tumbled off the desk.

Another shot echoed through the room.

I pulled myself back to my feet as Steve raced forward to help Kiera. But then John pushed himself up, gun in hand, and stared across towards the rack computer. A look of regret crossed his face and the gun tumbled to the ground. He gripped his chest and a stream of blood welled up between his fingers as he collapsed.

Kiera, grimacing, knelt upwards and lowered a pistol.

No one spoke, our shock filling the room, watching as Kiera took John's pulse.

At last, she shook her head. 'He's gone.'

I stared at the blood spreading out in a glistening dark pool beneath his body and a sob broke from somewhere deep inside me.

Steve gently held my shoulders and guided me away as Kiera covered John's head with her jacket. 'It'll be OK,' he said.

I wish I could have believed that, but every fibre of my being told me that this situation was only going to get worse. After all, John wasn't operating alone and, judging by the on-going firefight outside, we'd only delayed the inevitable.

Kiera withdrew extra ammo clips from John's jacket pocket. Then her gaze narrowed on the side of his head and she leant in and withdrew a flesh-coloured earbud from his ear.

'This isn't MI5 issue,' she said. Her gaze swivelled towards the control-room window. 'This must be how John has been keeping in contact with his friends out there. It also that means that they almost certainly know everything we do about Sentinel.' She shook her head. 'All these years, and we had no idea that he was a sleeper agent.'

'So why blow his cover now?' Graham asked.

'Presumably because his employers believe Sentinel is a high enough value target to warrant it.'

'And his employers are?' I asked.

'I have a reasonable idea, but it's far safer for you all that you don't know.' Kiera crossed to one of the landline phones, picked it up and frowned. 'And of course they've already cut the lines to the outside world. No wonder John was so keen to gather up all our mobiles. We have no way of calling for backup.'

'So what are we going to do?' Graham asked.

'Try to stay alive somehow and that means we begin to negotiate. After all, we have something they want.' She slipped John's earbud device into her ear. 'Hello, this is Kiera Roberts, MI5 field operations director, and I'd like to discuss a ceasefire.'

Her brow creased as she listened to the person on the other end.

'And you should also be clear that if you attempt to storm the control room I will not hesitate to destroy the computer system that contains the Sentinel AI code,' Kiera replied. She walked to the corner of the room and dropped her voice to a whisper as she continued to talk.

Static roared up again from the speakers.

'I think Sentinel is trying to get your attention, Lauren,' Steve said.

I turned, trying to slow the thumping of my heart, and gazed into the webcam. 'Go ahead, Sentinel.'

Symbols unfolded in my vision like yellow flowers opening in time-lapse. A memory rose from the depths of my mind...

I'd been training for the London Marathon and it had been beyond intense. I'd pounded the pavements night after night and mile after mile. At the start the distance I'd set myself to conquer seemed like a hopeless fantasy. But I'd clung on to my dream and built my fitness until I knew I could nail the distance. And it had been that same stubbornness that had eventually carried me all the way across the finish line one wonderful cold sunny morning with thousands of other marathon runners. The memory faded away along with the symbols.

Graham peered at me. 'And?'

'Sentinel seems to have zeroed in on the time I was training for the London Marathon.'

'So what do you think that means?' Steve asked.

'That Sentinel's equally determined to do something.'

'But what?' Steve replied.

'If only we had a simpler way of communicating with him than using Lauren's memories to guess at his emotions and yes and no answers,' Graham said.

Steve stared at him. 'But that's it! Lauren, why don't we ask Sentinel the equivalent of twenty questions?'

'You mean boil it down to just yes and no questions?'

'Precisely. The fact that Sentinel seems to understand what we're saying and can respond to you with symbols means that if we ask him the right questions we can create a more precise way to communicate with him.'

Hope started to bubble up inside me. 'That could really work, Steve.' I concentrated once more on the webcam. 'Sentinel, if you can understand me, show me a green triangle.'

The static became a simple drumbeat. My heart caught as a single green triangle rippled into existence, overlaid on top of my view of the control room.

'And?' Graham asked.

'So far so good, but let me check that wasn't a fluke.' I leant in again. 'Sentinel, we're trying to create a simple way to communicate with you. A green triangle means yes and a red square means no. Do you understand?'

A green triangle shimmered into existence.

I whooped. 'Steve, you utter genius.'

He beamed at me. 'Fantastic.'

'Now, let's find out more about this dark energy whilst we still have time,' Graham said.

I glanced across at Kiera – grim-faced as she continued her conversation with the person at the other of the line. How long did we have before the guys outside overpowered the last of Kiera's people and stormed this place? For all we knew, how the next few minutes played out might just alter the entire path of human history. And if there was even a tiny thing that I could do to make sure this worked out as it should, I'd do it – whatever it took and whatever the cost.

CHAPTER TEN

KIERA PULLED the earbud out and threw it across the room as fresh gunfire erupted outside.

'I take it negotiations have gone sour?' Graham asked.

Kiera glowered at him as she rushed to the door and began to heave a desk across it. 'Less stating the bleeding obvious please, and I'd appreciate more help building a barricade if you don't all want to die.'

'On my way,' Graham said. He turned to us. 'You two concentrate on getting some answers from Sentinel.'

'OK,' I said.

Graham dipped his chin towards us and raced over to help Kiera drag another desk towards the door.

I focused on nothing else but the camera in front of me. 'Sentinel, have you come to this world to help us?'

A single green triangle appeared in my vision. I nodded at Steve.

'Good going, so next question,' he said.

'And does the dark energy source that you're looking for represent some sort of threat to us?'

Green triangle.

'So can you stop that threat?'

A green triangle and red square appeared side by side.

'That was a yes/no reply,' I said.

'Then ask Sentinel if there is anything we can do to help him succeed,' he said.

Before I could even frame the question, a green triangle was floating in my vision. 'That's a big fat yes to your question so it seems like he can hear you too.'

'But how do we work out what it is?' Steve asked.

'I think I have an idea of how to narrow it down,' I replied. 'Sentinel, is it something we can do now from within this control room?'

Green triangle.

I turned to Steve. 'That was another yes.'

'OK, let's see if we can figure this out,' he said. 'Sentinel is an AI who has just downloaded himself into that computer. And then...' His eyes widened.

My mind raced to where Steve was headed with this line of reasoning. 'John sandboxed Sentinel on the MI5 computer when he thought he was a virus. And he did that by cutting Sentinel's ability to contact the outside world.'

'Which also made it easier for John to secure Sentinel for his employers.'

'So following on from that train of thought, Sentinel can't complete his mission until we set him free.'

Our gazes snapped to the network rack where the blue cables had been ripped out by John to isolate Sentinel's code.

I brought my face closer to the camera. 'You want us to plug you back in to the internet, don't you, Sentinel?'

A huge green triangle pulsed in my vision and I gave Steve an excited nod.

With a crack of glass a bullet punched a hole through the control-room window and thudded into the rear wall.

'Keep your heads down!' Kiera shouted. 'They must have a sniper hiding somewhere up on Lovell.' She threw a last chair at the top of her and Graham's makeshift barricade.

Steve and I flung ourselves flat to the floor as the others started crawling towards us.

'Sentinel needs access to the internet to complete his mission,' I said.

'But they cut the lines to the outside world,' Steve replied.

'Actually there may be another way,' Graham said as he and Kiera reached us. 'There's an old wired connection to the phone exchange that was left in place as a backup, before our connection was upgraded to an optical one to increase bandwidth. They may know enough about the optical connection to cut it, but I bet they don't know about the older line that runs to a different exchange.'

'Fantastic – so how do we use it?' Steve asked.

'Plug into any of the old grey Ethernet sockets. There's one under the main control desk below the window.'

'So what are we waiting for?' I said.

Kiera frowned at me. 'But we still have no way of knowing what Sentinel's going to do if we let him loose.'

'Will you listen to yourself, Kiera?' Steve said. 'Everything that Sentinel has done so far hasn't been hostile. And if I'm certain of anything, it's that he's capable of giving us more grief that we could ever handle, if he had hostile intentions. So as far as I'm concerned this alien AI really has come in peace and is here to help humanity.'

'Steve's right,' I said. 'You've got to see sense here, Kiera. Yes, I know it's a risk letting him out on to the internet, but it's also a calculated risk. We need to do this, because the alternative could be so much worse: letting him fall into their hands.'

The static roared up again and a green triangle flared into existence in my vision. 'And Sentinel agrees too,' I added.

Kiera peered at me. 'You're asking me to make a huge leap of faith here.'

'Please trust me on this. I've never been so sure about anything in my life.' And somehow I really was.

Kiera stared at the ceiling, an MI5 operative in an impossible situation. What would I do in her place if asked to make this kind of decision?

She finally shook her head. 'I just can't allow you to do that.'

Before I could answer, a spray of bullets shattered the control-room window and drummed into the wall, destroying several framed prints of deep space subjects.

Kiera reacted instantly, popping up and returning gunfire through the remnants of the window. As she started to duck down again she yelped as a spray of blood erupted from her left shoulder. She crumpled to the ground.

Graham, keeping his head down, opened her jacket to reveal a large red bloodstain soaking her white shirt over the area of her shoulder. 'You've been wounded, Kiera.'

She looked up at him through slitted eyes. 'No shit, Sherlock!' She winced and gritted her teeth as she grabbed Graham's arm. 'Listen to me. Whatever you do, make sure that Sentinel doesn't fall into their hands. You must destroy our computer that contains his core code.' She gestured towards her gun. 'Take my gun – you're going to have to defend yourselves against the people who are about to storm this place.'

'But even if we destroy your computer, there's every chance they'll still be able to retrieve the code to reconstruct him,' Steve said.

'There's no other alternative,' Kiera replied.

'You know there is,' I said.

Kiera stared up at me, a dozen emotions passing through her

expression, as Graham threw open a first-aid box and began to bandage her shoulder.

I could now only hear a single pistol outside, responding to the continuing blasts of automatic fire. One single MI5 agent couldn't hold out much longer against that sort of opposition.

And then Kiera nodded. 'They're going to sack me anyway for cocking this mission up, so go ahead and pray that this is the right call, Lauren.'

'I'm certain of it,' I replied.

'OK, the one thing we must do the moment you get us online again is call for backup,' Kiera replied.

'You've got it.'

I edged across to the network rack and took hold of the dangling blue cable that John had ripped out. I crawled under the desk and spotted a dusty grey socket. With everything mentally crossed, I plugged the wire in.

When I emerged back out from beneath the control desk, I saw the others staring at the screens. The scrolling numbers had vanished from every one of them.

Steve had his hands on his head as Graham plugged a laptop into the rack and placed it into Kiera's lap.

'Come on, Sentinel, get on with whatever it is you have to do,' Steve said,

The monitors all went blank and I held my breath. Then different webpages suddenly filled every display in the control room.

Graham stared at the monitor nearest him. 'That looks like the website for the Pentagon.'

Steve gawped at the large screen in the middle of the room. 'And that's the Russian Ministry of Defence site.'

All the screens blinked again as they reloaded with fresh pages, this time with websites for power utility companies. That was followed by the details of research papers, from space projects to obscure branches of quantum physics. Countless sites of every description began to accelerate past.

Steve whistled. 'Now that's what I call an internet search.'

We watched as hundreds of websites flashed across the monitors at an impossible speed despite the old connection to the exchange. Occasionally a screen would slow long enough for me to be able to almost read it. I started to spot top-secret banners across many of the pages, most of which were filled with complex-looking diagrams, each stamped with the insignias of Russia, America, Great Britain, China or other countries.

'I'm as sure as I can be that's Sentinel accessing highly classified data,' Kiera said through clenched teeth as she typed on the laptop. 'And for that to happen means Sentinel has hacked past the highest levels of government encryption. So I just hope you're right about his intentions, Lauren.'

'I'm certain of it.'

Steve pointed at a monitor. 'Holy shit, will you look at this?'

Diagrams for what could only be described as UFOs, varying from classic disc-shaped crafts to V-shaped delta flying wings, sped past.

If I'd had my phone on me I could have taken pictures to analyse later... 'Steve, where's the camera we use for the publicity shots?'

'In my desk.' He crawled over to it, reached up and rifled through his drawer. He withdrew a compact Sony camera and lobbed it over to me. 'Knock yourself out.'

I powered the camera on and began taking photos as quickly as I could, capturing dozens of craft. It wasn't long before I realised that one in particular kept cropping up, a design I hadn't seen anywhere in the movies or anywhere else for that matter. All the shots were blurry images of an inverted tetrahedron, a three sided pyramid shape. According to the location stamps on the images, these had been taken from a dozen sites around the world.

'This is a conspiracist's wet dream,' Steve said, shaking his head.

'The truth is quite literally out there,' I replied.

'Oh bloody hell,' Kiera said, staring at her laptop's screen.

'What now?' I asked.

'It looks as though John was busy before he died. It seems as if he released a worm virus that has taken MI5's systems offline. And that means I can't communicate with Control through the normal channels.'

'But there must be another way of getting a message to your people? Or to anyone who could help us?'

'What do you want me to do, call 999?'

'If that's what it bloody takes. Use an online email account – anything you have to get us help.'

Kiera scowled but started typing again.

The websites racing past on the screens started to slow and I began to see the same phrase across multiple pages: 'Dark Energy'.

'Looks as if Sentinel is closing in on the scent of whatever he's after,' Steve said.

Then the images slowed to a stop, and each and every monitor had exactly the same page on it:

'Engineering plans for the Dark Energy Collector (DEC). Prototype design by Professor Martin Stevens.'

My heart caught and I peered at the camera. 'Is this it, Sentinel? Is this what you were looking for?'

A green triangle blossomed like a firework in my sight.

I leant back in my chair. 'This is it, everyone.' I took a final photo and then slipped the memory card out from the camera and under the strap of my woven leather bracelet.

Kiera gave me a questioning look as she continued to type.

'If we die at least there's a chance that someone else will learn what Sentinel has been searching for and maybe do something about it,' I said.

'Let's hope it doesn't come to that,' she replied.

Steve peered at the schematics of the DEC experiment – it consisted of a sphere surrounded by electrodes. 'This looks like some sort of experimental system designed to detect dark energy.'

A fresh spray of bullets peppered the room.

Kiera handed her gun to Graham. 'You need to return fire.'

'Me, since when?'

'Somebody needs to.'

'OK.'

Graham closed his eyes as he raised his hand over the lip of the window and fired the pistol until he'd emptied the clip. He breathed hard as bullets riddled the control room, taking out the large screen in a shower of sparks.

'Good man,' Kiera said as she closed the laptop.

'How did you get on with calling the cavalry?' Steve asked.

'I've just sent an email to a secure server. It should take around thirty minutes for backup to get here.'

'That sounds like a hell of a long time to me in our current situation,' Graham said.

'Well, that's how long we have to hold out for,' Kiera said. Grimacing, she took the gun from him, reloaded it and handed it back.

Every screen in the room blinked again and large numbers appeared on each display.

100

99

98...

'Is this some sort of countdown?' I said.

Steve peered up at the network rack. 'That thing lit up like a

Christmas tree suggests a large amount of data is being uploaded...'

I looked back at the webcam. 'You're uploading yourself and going after this DEC experiment, aren't you, Sentinel?'

Green triangle.

I nodded to the others.

'So when the timer gets to zero there'll be nothing left for those guys out there to grab,' Steve said.

'So we just need to keep them out of here for a little bit longer,' Kiera said.

Graham sent another volley of shots over the window ledge with the reloaded gun.

The gunfire fell silent outside.

'Either you're the luckiest shot on the planet, Graham, or that's not a good sign at all,' Steve said.

'The latter, I'm afraid,' said Kiera. 'It sounds as if the last of my colleagues have been taken out, which almost certainly means they're going to attempt to storm this control room next.'

I looked at the people around me. In a few minutes we could all be dead. OK, so I could just accept that, or I could try to do something to swing the odds a fraction in our favour.

I crossed to John's body, keeping low, and picked up his pistol, which was lying beside him.

Half the lights on the network tower blinked out as the timer became stuck at thirty-one.

Steve hissed. 'That looks as if they just discovered our old internet connection.'

'So that's it? Sentinel is stuck in here with us?' I asked.

'It looks like it,' Kiera said.

'And there is no way backup will get here in time now,' Graham said.

Kiera gestured towards the MI5 computer system. 'Pull the

hard disks out of that thing and do your best to destroy them.' She began to reload the pistol with a fresh clip.

Steve gave me a grim look as he grabbed a screwdriver and crossed to the MI5 computers.

Tears beaded my eyes. We were about to destroy a sentient being that had come to our world to help humanity. Quite the welcome mat. 'Please don't do this, Steve.'

'But we have to, Lauren,' he replied. 'It's the only play left open to us.'

Graham reached out to take the reloaded gun from Kiera, but she gritted her teeth and waved him away. 'I'll take it from here.' She gazed at all of us. 'OK, listen up. This is how it will probably work out from here. I'm certain we're dealing with highly trained individuals. Their mission will be to retrieve Sentinel intact, which means they will lob a flashbang in here first to disorientate us. The effects of that will last around fifteen seconds, but try not to look directly at the flash and cover your ears when it detonates. Even so, we will still be affected, to a certain extent, and they'll attack the control room whilst we're recovering.' She rested the pistol on her knee and aimed it at the door.

Even with Kiera in here with us, and although she hadn't said it, I knew we didn't stand a chance against the highly trained soldiers out there.

Steve, his hands shaking, began to unscrew the retaining rail of the MI5 rack computer.

I raised John's gun and pointed it towards the door as acid swirled through my stomach.

Whether we lived or died would all come down to this.

CHAPTER ELEVEN

I TRIED to ignore the drumbeat of my own fear as I held on to that gun. A frozen moment in time, waiting for the end of all my dreams, all my everythings. When the black metal canister finally tumbled through the shattered control-room window and bounced across the floor, it almost felt like a relief.

'Flashbang!' Kiera shouted.

My adrenalin spiked and I flew myself flat, bringing up my hands to cover my ears, but I closed my eyes a fraction too late.

A pulse of light blazed through the room, searing my vision to white, and was accompanied by a deafening bang. A stinging concussion wave slapped into my face. As an afterglow sun flooded my vision, my ears rang with a squealing pitch.

I tried to push myself up, but the floor swayed under me, the blast affecting my balance. Yet even as my head throbbed with a migraine-level headache my hearing started to return.

A clonking noise was coming from somewhere. I turned towards the source of the sound as it was answered by the crack of pistol fire. My vision slowly started to return too, and I began to make out the control-room door being slammed into one of the desks of our makeshift barricade.

A hand appeared round the door and Kiera squeezed off another shot. The hand snatched back.

But how were the others doing?

I scanned the room, every muscle in my neck aching, to see Graham gasping for breath. Nearby, Steve had vomited over the floor and was wiping the corner of his mouth with his hand. Then I spotted a dark shape beyond them, climbing through the shattered window. The man raised his semi-automatic weapon towards Kiera, whose attention was still focused on the door.

I fumbled for my own gun, which I'd dropped, found it and raised my shaking hand to aim it at the intruder as his green laser dot danced across Kiera's back. The pistol kicked in my hand and a sickening spray of blood erupted from his head. With a muffled grunt the guy pitched backwards out of the window.

An overwhelming feeling of nausea came over me and I dropped the gun, driving my fingernails into my palm as tears instantly filled my eyes. What the hell had I done?

Kiera spun round and stared at the smoking gun in front of me and then at the window. 'Keep it together, Lauren – I need your backup.'

I managed a vague nod in return.

The door banged against the barricade, but far harder this time. The pile of desks and chairs began to squeal backwards over the floor and two figures wearing balaclavas squeezed through the gap in the door. Kiera's pistol cried out to meet them.

Steve crossed to me and picked up the gun. 'Do you want me to take over, Lauren?'

'No, I've got this.'

He nodded, no argument, and, maybe understanding me better than I did myself at this precise moment, handed me the pistol.

My body numb, I raised the gun and aimed at one of the two guys. I breathed out and fired.

A bullet hole appeared in the wall just over the lead guy's head as he ducked and swept automatic weapon fire towards me.

Steve and I dropped flat to the floor as the hailstorm of bullets ricocheted off the filing cabinets and flew into the ceiling, showering us in plaster dust.

Graham hunkered down behind the network rack and shot me a wide-eyed look, his lips pulled back over his teeth. He looked as terrified as I felt.

We were outgunned and outmatched – scientists, not soldiers, who hadn't asked for any of this. And what was this all for anyway? If those guys got hold of Sentinel, what would happen then? Would he simply end up stacked in some vast *Indiana-Jones*-type warehouse that was full of secrets we weren't meant to know about? Or would he be picked apart and analysed like a lab rat? Meanwhile, the AI's mission to help humanity would be flushed down the toilet.

Something hardened inside me. *Screw this!*

I leant round the corner of the desk and fired off a volley of shots at the soldiers until my pistol was clicking on empty.

Kiera, tucked behind a control station, threw me another clip. She made a pantomime of releasing the clip on the side of her own gun and sliding a fresh one in. I mimicked her actions, ejecting my empty one and reloading too.

'Talk about on-the-job training,' Steve said.

I could even manage a hint of a smile.

Kiera wordlessly mouthed to me, 'One, two, three, go...'

Both of us leapt up and opened fire on the men who'd begun to climb over the barrier. One of them crumpled across a desk, but the other backed out whilst shooting wildly and destroying the monitor just above Graham's head.

Temporary silence filled the control room.

I found myself staring at the man draped over the remains of the barricade like someone who'd tried to storm a trench in the First World War. My heart clenched. Had I killed him too, or had it been Kiera? And did it really matter? Either way I would carry the scars of this night for as long as I lived, which might not be that long anyway.

Someone was shaking me... Steve.

Graham gestured towards the control-room window. 'Look!'

I became aware of distant shouts from outside. Then I realised that Lovell's dish was moving, the whine of its motors filling the night air. It slowed to a stop, its dish aiming towards a point near its zenith.

My eyes focused on the text of one of the few remaining monitors.

Target selected: communication satellite, Varuna. Countdown restarted. Thirty seconds...

Steve punched the air. 'Oh, you complete beauty, Sentinel!'

'I don't understand,' Kiera said.

'After they cut the landlines, I think Sentinel found an alternative way out of here.'

Graham slouched against a filing cabinet. 'You mean he's uploading himself to this Inmarsat-4 satellite?'

'I think so, which means he's converted Lovell from a receiver to a transmitter.' Steve chucked away his screwdriver. 'I won't be needing that any more.'

20

19

18...

Fresh hope burned inside me like a tiny flame. 'So if we manage to hold them off for a bit longer, there will be nothing left for them to take?'

Kiera gazed at us from across the control room. 'Even if that's true, it won't stop those guys out there murdering all of us. They won't want any witnesses to what happened here tonight.'

'So we're damned if Sentinel escapes and damned if he doesn't?' Graham asked.

'I'm afraid so,' Kiera replied.

I massaged my fingers into my neck, trying to unknot the muscles that were still tense from the flashbang... 'So a *Butch Cassidy and the Sundance Kid* shoot-out it is.'

Kiera gave me a genuine smile that reached her eyes. 'I've always loved that old movie, but less so the ending.'

She might have been a hard-faced bitch, but I was starting to like this woman. 'Yeah, me too.'

Kiera tossed me another gun clip. 'That's the end of our ammunition, I'm afraid.'

'Then let's make every one of our bullets count.' I reloaded my weapon with more ease this time.

Kiera gave me an approving look. 'You really should consider a career in MI5.'

I gestured towards her clothes. 'Not a huge fan of the trouser-suit uniform, thanks all the same.'

Kiera laughed. 'This look certainly isn't for everyone.' She cocked her pistol, face deadly serious again. 'Once our friends outside have regrouped they'll attack again.'

Steve gave me a sideways glance.

'What?' I asked him.

'You seem to have turned into our very own Lara Croft, that's all.'

'I *wish*, although I do think I could seriously pull off the sassy shorts look.'

'You really are my sort of woman.'

'I realised that a long while ago, Steve, but now is not the time for that particular discussion.'

He gave me a sad smile and shrugged.

Yes, a hopeless fantasy for another life.

10

9

8...

A green canister blurred through the broken window and rolled across the floor.

'That's a smoke grenade! Keep low to the floor and cover your mouth,' Kiera called out.

With a hiss smoke erupted from the canister and started to fill the room. Within seconds dense vapour was scratching my throat and making my lungs burn.

I heard the control-room door bang open again and this time green laser lines skewered the fog now filling the room.

As Kiera and I fired blindly towards the source, the next moment seemed to happen in slow motion. One of the light lines locked on to Kiera and automatic gunfire tore into her. Without any form of body armour she didn't stand a chance.

Kiera jerked backwards, red stains blossoming across her white shirt.

My gun tumbled from my hand and I raced to help her, no longer caring about my fate.

The guy at the head of the group shouted something to the other men and held up a clenched fist.

All of that was a blur to me.

I reached Kiera, who was gasping hard for breath, and gently cradled her head into my lap. Her eyes rolled to meet mine. There was no fear in them, only acceptance. She'd fought the good fight and lost, a warrior till the end.

Steve and Graham raised their hands as green laser sights danced over their chests.

The leader of the assault team walked towards us calmly, his pistol pointing at me. I glowered up at him and stared into the piercing glacier-blue eyes behind his goggles. I dimly registered a crescent scar radiating out from his left eye.

I would die rather than give this man the satisfaction of seeing the fear that was churning inside me.

I raised up my chin at the man. 'You can fuck right off!'

His gaze held mine: crystal lakes of ice. Then he raised his arm and dropped it. Instantly he and his men sighted their weapons on us.

No witnesses...

The leader scowled and glanced towards the shattered control-room window.

And then I heard the whirring noise of helicopter rotor blades growing louder and faster. The leader looked at me for a moment longer, then across at the computer on which Sentinel had been installed.

The flame inside me grew fiercer. *This is not how I die!*

In the split second that he looked away I leapt sideways and rolled towards the gun I'd dropped. I grabbed it and bounced back to my feet as a stream of bullets swept past me. I might not have been trained for this, but adrenalin was powering me on.

I aimed at the man nearest me, fired, rolled sideways and fired again.

Both men crumpled to the ground.

And the leader?

I swung my pistol around at the spot where he'd been standing a second ago. I caught sight of him disappearing out of the door carrying the MI5 computer. My gaze tore to the one remaining operational monitor screen.

Data upload complete.

I sagged as Steve and Graham slowly lowered their hands.

Steve stared at me. 'Holy shit, Lauren, where did that come from?'

'I think I was channelling the spirit of Lara Croft for a moment there.'

A wild wind swept into the control room from the rotor wash, and the remnants of the smoke were blown away. Outside, a twin-rotored Chinook settled in to land. The moment it touched down, figures darted down its rear ramp and stared to creep towards the control room, guns raised.

I crossed back to Kiera, whose whole body was convulsing. Her eyes locked on to mine, her voice the quietest murmur.

I put my ear closer to catch her faint words. 'What are you trying to tell me, Kiera?'

'Overseers...' she whispered. She blinked hard. 'Stop them...' Her eyes rolled. With a long sigh she stilled and a trickle of blood ran from the corner of her mouth.

Tears ran down my cheeks as I cupped her face with my hand.

Steve crouched by my side. 'What did she say, Lauren?'

I stared at him for a moment, already knowing the information that Kiera had just shared with me was going to change the rest of my life. And I also knew in an instant there was no way that I could inflict the danger of that knowledge on my friends. Friends who'd already gone through too much.

'I didn't catch it,' I replied, my voice tight.

The door burst open and the soldiers I'd watched disembark in combat gear rushed inside.

'Drop your weapon!' one of the men shouted.

It took me a moment to realise he was talking to me. I threw the pistol away across the room.

'Hands above your heads!'

I just stared at him as Graham and Steve complied.

A tall man, with blond hair peeking out from beneath his helmet, emerged from the group and walked towards me gun in hand. He peered down at Kiera's lifeless body in my lap. Then he looked at me for the longest moment before pocketing his gun.

Three of his men darted forward and secured our hands behind our backs with plastic ties.

The blond guy looked at me with hazel eyes. 'My name is Captain Jacobs. Would someone please tell me what the bloody hell has happened here?'

Graham glowered at him. 'We were bloody attacked obviously! But I thought it was going to take thirty minutes for you guys to get here – not that I'm complaining.'

'I don't know what you're talking about,' Captain Jacobs replied.

'I thought Kiera told you everything when she called for backup?'

'Kiera who?' the captain replied.

I gestured with my chin to her body. 'That incredibly brave MI5 woman who just sacrificed her life to save us.'

'I don't know anything about that. The only reason we're here is that someone at this facility hacked one of our most secure military satellites and sent a distress signal calling for urgent help.'

My eyes tore to the monitor. *Data upload complete.*

'Sentinel did that knowing the others wouldn't get here in time.'

Graham nodded. 'He saved us.'

'Is that the name of your hacker?' the captain asked.

Steve smiled. 'All I can say is that our debriefing is going take a very long time.'

The first rays of dawn were starting to tint the sky along the eastern horizon as the chaos of soldiers and MI5 personnel dealt with the aftermath of what had happened. Graham had volunteered to continue with the questioning to give Steve and me a break, as they'd already questioned the two of us non-stop for four hours. Apart from feeling exhausted on every level, I also needed time to think.

We sat in silence at one of the picnic tables in the viewing area outside as we tried to emotionally process what had occurred whilst people hurried past. A tiny point of light crawled overhead – one of thousands of satellites that circled Earth.

'I wonder how Sentinel is getting on up there,' Steve said.

'I hope he's already downloaded himself from Varuna and is starting to deal with the DEC experiment threat,' I replied.

'Whatever he's doing, I wish him luck with it. Anything that's important enough for an alien AI to travel from a parallel dimension to tackle it has to be pretty damn serious.' Steve looked up at Lovell, its white steel struts being kissed by the golden dawn. 'Things are never going to be the same again, are they?'

'Nothing can be after what we learnt tonight. This changes everything and it's certainly changed what matters to me.' The satellite disappeared into the growing glow on the horizon. 'And I'm really going to miss this place.'

Steve's forehead creased. 'What do you mean, Lauren?'

'I mean that I'm not going to stop till I get to the truth and that will mean hitting the road.'

'So you're going to join the ranks of the UFO hunter crazies?'

'I suppose so, although now we do know they're not that crazy.'

'But you've told me a hundred times that working here is your dream job. You can't throw your career away over this, however important you think it is.'

'Actually I can. The fact that aliens are visiting our world takes priority even over my dream job.'

'I suppose I can see that. But what will you do?'

'To start with I want to visit the locations where those blurry photos of inverted pyramid craft were taken. I'm going to find eyewitnesses to go on record.'

'So our very own Fox Mulder then?'

'Something like that.'

Steve peered at me. 'And why should this be your personal mission, Lauren? It could be extremely dangerous, you know?'

'Because I watched Kiera die protecting us and I want to make the people responsible pay for that. Also, if UFOs really have been buzzing our skies on a regular basis, then people have a right to know.'

Steve shook his head. 'Something tells me that you might just be the person to crack this conspiracy wide open, with the determination and drive you have.'

'And don't forget my winning personality.'

He snorted. 'You know that dream job of yours will always be here for you, Lauren.'

'Always great to have a fantastic plan B.'

'And you'll keep in contact?'

'Of course. You're not going to get rid of me that easily, Steve.'

He smiled. 'Good to know.'

The control-room door was opened and held by Captain Jacobs as two of his soldiers carried a stretcher outside bearing a body. A blanket was pulled up over the head but a white-shirted arm lay exposed to one side of the body. Kiera.

I stood up and approached Jacobs. 'Do you mind if I see her one last time?'

His eyes lingered on me. 'Of course not.' He nodded to his two men who halted.

With my heart hammering hard I peeled back the blanket to reveal Kiera's face. Her eyes were still open and filled with serenity. I drank in the strength that still lingered in her expression. If I had half the determination of this woman, I would be doing well.

I leant down and whispered into her ear, 'I'll stop them,

Kiera...' I gently placed my fingers on her eyelids and drew them closed. Then a tremble ran through me and I bit back a sob.

Jacobs pulled the blanket back over her head, then dipped his chin towards me. He and his men moved away with Kiera's body towards a military ambulance.

Steve's hand appeared on my shoulder. 'Are you OK, Lauren?'

'No, not really.'

He pulled me into a tight hug. The warmth of his body ebbed into mine and I started to shake.

Steve kissed my head gently and tears flooded my vision.

There was so much I wanted to talk to him about, but I couldn't. Who exactly were the Overseers and why had they tried to suppress the truth about UFO encounters for all these years? To stop the general public panicking? Or was there a darker reason for all of this? Whatever the future held, I already knew that I would need to do it solo. It wasn't so much because of whom I could trust, but because I wasn't prepared to put anyone else in danger.

I wrapped my arms tighter round Steve's neck. The edge of the blue memory card peeked out from beneath my leather bracelet. I peered up at the last bright star in the sky, watching the giant red Betelgeuse fading into the growing dawn over Lovell. And in the light of that new day I made a promise to myself. Whatever the cost, I'd never stop, not until I'd unearthed the truth.

LINKS

Do please leave that all important review for **The Signal** here: https://geni.us/TheSignal

So now you've finished **The Signal,** are you ready for the next page-turning instalment in the series?

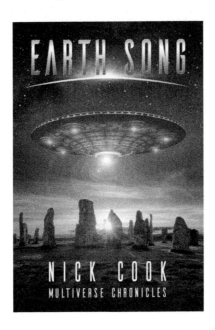

A year has passed since the events of **The Signal** and alerts are erupting across the international UFO forums about a new alien phenomenon.

In her search for answers, Lauren teams up with archaeologist Jack Harper. Can they unlock an ancient secret buried in Orkney to defend Earth against a threat set to extinguish life on our planet for ever?

The Earth Song series is available on Kindle, in paperback and free

within KU Unlimited. You can buy Earth Song here: https://
geni.us/EarthSongSeries

OTHER BOOKS BY NICK COOK

Prequel to the Multiverse Chronicles

The Earth Song Series (The Multiverse Chronicles)

The Fractured Light Trilogy (The Multiverse Chronicles)

AFTERWORD

First and foremost, I hoped you enjoyed *The Signal*. If you have the time please do take a moment to leave a review. If you're wondering why this is so important, reviews are the best way to spread the word about a book. People are also much more likely to buy a book that have more reviews than just a few, so leaving a review is great help to me as an author. Here is the Amazon link to leave a review: https://geni.us/TheSignal

So now hopefully *The Signal* has wetted your appetite to explore my Multiverse Chronicles further. Right now if you haven't read any of my work previously you stand at a fork in the road with my books. You could now follow Lauren's journey and her search for the truth about UFOs as she tries to expose the Overseers for what they are. If so, you will want to read *Earth Song* next, book one in the *Earth Song* series. Alternatively, waiting for you is my *Fractured Light* trilogy. This follows Sentinel's journey and the reason behind his arrival in our world. If you're a fan of Stranger Things and Fringe, then this trilogy should be right up your street. Of course, as the author, I'd recommend you read both series!

The link for *Earth Song* is here: https://geni.us/EarthSong

And here's the link for *Fractured light*: https://geni.us/FracturedLightAmazon

The inspiration for *The Signal* story actually came from, of all things, a book trailer I produced for my publisher for *Cloud Riders*. In it, a strange signal has been received at Jodrell Bank, a site I visited to capture video footage for the trailer. And that visit left a lasting impression on me until that itch turned into the book you have just read. If you want to see that trailer, you can check it out here: Cloud Riders trailer.

If you visit my website – http://www.nick-cook.net – you'll quickly realise I have a lifelong love affair with all things space, something I blame on growing up during the era of the Apollo moon landings. That not only led to my passion for science fiction but also my love of astronomy. If you want to be the first to know about my new releases and to find out behind-the-scenes info, if you haven't already, I recommend you sign up to my newsletter on my website, or via this link: https://www.subscribepage.com/s6z3s9_copy

The question of alien civilisations is one that I feel has to be true logistically, not least due to the sheer size of the universe and existence of other planets that could sustain life. Whether craft have visited this world or not is a subject of debate and something I have no expertise on other than willing it to be true. Yet I do have experience of witnessing something strange one night...

In 2008, I was a member of an astronomy group that arranged a viewing session on a remote site near Cley Hill in Wiltshire, England, a location famed for UFO sightings. In all honesty, I'd previously taken these sightings with a very big pinch of proverbial salt. However, on the night of the meeting, the twenty experienced amateur astronomers gathered there, including me, witnessed something that can only be described as strange.

A bright point of light appeared at low altitude (around a thousand metres) with no visible exhaust trail and moving in total silence. It was travelling from east to west, between us and the horizon, at a relatively slow speed (maybe around seventy-five miles per hour). Initially, because of our proximity to Salisbury Plain which is a military training area, we thought it was a helicopter, but no navigation lights were visible (as a former pilot, I know what to look for). One of our group managed to align a scope on it long enough to confirm that they couldn't see navigation lights even through the magnification. Yet at this point we didn't think it was that unusual apart from the fact we couldn't hear any rotor or engine noise at all. But it was what happened next that was really weird.

When that point of light reached a position parallel to us, it started noiselessly accelerating until it disappeared over the horizon in around twenty seconds...and that's seriously fast for any aircraft.

We all looked at each other and then someone said, 'Did we just see a UFO?' There was much nervous laughter.

To this day, I have no idea what we witnessed that night. Maybe it was an experimental secret craft or maybe something stranger. Whatever it was in the sky that night, it was witnessed by a group of experienced astronomers who are used to seeing the usual candidates for UFOs – the planet Venus, fireballs, even lenticular clouds, and so on. What we'd seen was none of those things. Queue spooky music.

Whilst I was writing *The Signal*, the Pentagon's secret UFO monitoring programme was revealed, the footage of which is compelling and worth watching, and you may have spotted I included a reference to it in this story. You can find the video interview of Luis Elizondo, former Pentagon military intelligence officer, here: YouTube interview.

I hope you check out *Earth Song* and *Fractured Light*. But remember, don't forget to watch the shadows because the darkness is coming for Earth.

If you're interested in reading *Earth Song* an extract from that book follows.

PROLOGUE TO EARTH SONG
ONE YEAR LATER - LOCATION, ORKNEY

THE CAR FERRY churned its way over the fog-covered sea, a foaming white trail eddying out across the water's surface. The icy mist numbed my face as the deck vibrated slightly through the soles of my walking boots.

The woman in the ticket office said the view of Orkney would be amazing as we approached. She said I would never forget my first sight of the island...

I peered ahead through the mist towards the sooty outline of land, screwing up my eyes as if hoping to develop X-ray vision, but the featureless grey fog still sucked the view away.

At the sound of a door closing behind me, I glanced round. An old man wearing an equally ancient and worn waterproof jacket had appeared on the deck. Earlier I'd seen him drive a knackered Saab on to the ferry. An unlit cigarette was glued to his lip by the power of saliva. He fumbled in his pocket and withdrew one of those old-fashioned flint lighters. A clunk and a click and a flame spluttered in the breeze long enough for him to light his rolled cigarette.

The guy pulled the collar of his jacket up as he took a long drag of the cigarette, which glowed like a hot coal. He let out a contented sigh as he ambled towards me across the empty deck.

Like always, my instinct flashed up a warning at his approach. Every stranger had to be treated with caution, especially since the car crash that had destroyed what remained of my old life.

The Overseers played dirty and I couldn't afford to take any chances.

I cast a subtle glance at the old guy. He seemed an unlikely recruit for the secret organisation – to my knowledge they favoured ex-military personnel. Besides, this wouldn't be the first innocent old guy to single me out. For reasons unknown to me, I seemed to be like catnip to them.

'Nice weather for it,' the man said in a warm Scottish accent as he neared.

'Yeah, sunlight is so overrated.'

He snorted. 'You're a tourist then?'

'Sort of.'

'Oh, I see. Well, Miss *Sort of Tourist*, you could've picked a better time of year to come than now.' He lifted his hand. 'I'm Patrick by the way.'

I shook his surprisingly warm hand, but I didn't offer up my own name. I, Lauren Stelleck, needed to keep off everyone's radar as much as possible, and that included revealing too much information.

Thankfully, Patrick didn't seem to be expecting me to reciprocate. Instead, he sucked on his cigarette and leant on the railing to peer out into the fog, seeming to settle for companionable silence. And with my crowded headspace at the moment, that was good.

The wind started to moan around us and, like curtains rolling back at a theatre, the fog swirled aside to reveal a looming cliff line. In front of it rose a huge pillar of rock surrounded by thousands of whirling seabirds. Even at this distance, I was almost certain that the dark birds with white chests, stubby wings and flappy flight paths were puffins.

'That view is quite something,' I said.

'The Old Man of Hoy is a grand old sight. And that whole area is a nature reserve.'

'It looks like something straight out of a *Jurassic Park* film,' I replied, allowing myself a brief smile towards this stranger.

'Sadly, you won't find any T-rexs roaming around there. Although that would be great for the tourists.'

'Maybe, but possibly less so for the birdlife, hey?'

He snorted. 'Aye, lass.'

The wind howled and whipped up the waves.

As the air started to turn bitter, Patrick took out a hip flask. 'Do you fancy a wee dram just to take the chill away?'

'A margarita is more my usual speed.'

'Maybe so, but you're here for new experiences, am I right?'

More than he realised. 'I guess I am.'

Patrick unscrewed the top of the flask, took a sip first and then handed it to me.

I held the flask for a moment. If by some miracle he was working for the Overseers, if the drink was spiked, he wouldn't have tried it first. No, on this occasion I could give my usual paranoia a short break.

I took a cautious sip and whisky fire tanged my tonsils. After the heat rush, the rich aftertaste hinted at peat and honey. The afterglow slipping down my throat was like someone had just turned a radiator on inside me – way better than porridge could ever manage. I wiped the top of the flask with my sleeve and handed it back to him.

'That's very smooth.'

'The finest single malt in all of Scotland, Orkney's very own Highland Park,' Patrick replied.

'I think I could develop a taste for it.'

He nodded. 'Whilst you're on the islands you most certainly will. It'll snare a part of your heart for ever.' He took another sip and gazed out towards Hoy.

'And you're a poet too.'

'We islanders are dreamers of every sort.'

I smiled at the mental image of a windswept island filled with hopeless romantics. The old Lauren would have fitted right in, the woman who viewed radio telescopes as a love poem from humanity to the cosmos. But that version of me had been lost six months ago when my aunt had died.

I'd been on the verge of giving up this whole business when a UFO sighting over Exmoor had caught my attention. After months of frustration, I'd decided to make one last-ditch attempt to capture evidence of a craft.

The crazy thing was, Aunt Lucy shouldn't have even been there. But she'd known how strung out I'd become whilst trying to prove that UFOs actually existed. She'd always supported me in every half-crazy dream that I'd set my heart on, even my brief attempt to be a singer in my early teens.

So she was with me for moral support as we drove along a twisty B-road through Exmoor one June day six months ago. A truck had appeared out of nowhere and rammed us from behind, forcing Aunt Lucy to lose control of her Mini. We'd crashed into a wall, but it was no accident. I knew that when a guy in black combat fatigues and a ski mask had emerged from the truck and headed towards us, a pistol in his hand.

As I'd been pinned in the crumpled Mini, I'd spotted the scar radiating from his left eye. I still remembered the cold feeling of dread that had unleashed. You see, I'd come across Mr Eye Scar before. Despite my broken arm, I'd tried to shield my aunt from what I'd known was coming.

In those last moments she'd whispered that she loved me as

she began to lose consciousness. Only then had I spotted the blood running down the side of her head from where her skull had hit the door frame.

A strange calm had filled me as I'd cradled my aunt and waited to die with her. I'd tried my best, but it was our time. Then in a split second everything had changed, when a police car had rounded the corner.

The assassin had stood stock-still for a whole second, the expression in his eyes wavering behind his mask. But then he'd run back to his truck and sped away. A police car had then screeched to a halt next to us and called for an ambulance.

But it'd been too late.

Less than a minute later, Aunt Lucy had died in my arms and my soul had shattered into a million pieces that would never be put back together.

There had been a helicopter search and temporary road-blocks across the moors, but the guy and his truck were never seen again. The police had run the truck's number plate, which had turned out to be fake – no surprise to me.

MI5 had later asked me about Mr Eye Scar. He'd led the assault team that'd stormed Jodrell Bank and murdered all those people that awful night. And the secret organisation he worked for? The Overseers, who among other things were behind the conspiracy of silence about the truth of UFOs. And they had killed my precious Aunt Lucy.

It had made this more personal than ever. I was even more determined to destroy the Overseers organisation and everything they stood for. And if I came across Mr Eye Scar again, nothing would be off the menu when it came to dishing out some well-deserved vengeance.

It was why I was here on a ferry bound for Orkney – chasing down the latest lead in my hunt for the truth.

My attention snapped back to reality as the ferry rolled down a deep trough in the waves and spray erupted over the boat. Patrick and I were doused with water as the ferry started to roll up the wave.

I shuddered as the weaknesses in my cagoule were found by watery fingers and my skin grew soaked. 'Shit, that's cold.'

Patrick raised an eyebrow at me. His waterproof dripped with seawater and his wet grey hair stuck to his head; he looked toasty warm with glowing red cheeks.

'Aye, it's getting a bit fresh,' he said. 'We may as well head back to the car deck. We'll be landing soon.'

'No car for me. I'm a foot passenger.'

'Are you now? Someone meeting you at the harbour?'

'No, I'm travelling solo for this trip. Is there Uber on Orkney?'

'Uber what?'

I smiled. 'Don't worry about it – I'll find a taxi.'

Patrick shook his head. 'No need, because I'm going to give you a lift.'

My honed survival instinct kicked in. Patrick might have looked like a harmless old man, but I hadn't managed to evade the Overseers since the crash by getting careless with strangers.

'Honestly, don't worry about it.'

'What, you think I may have wicked plans for you?' His mouth curled into a smile.

'No...but... Well, you know.' I raised a shoulder.

'You can't be too careful?'

'Sorry, just a bit wary about people I don't know.'

'I understand.' He sighed. 'Modern times, hey? Anyway, there's a taxi rank at the harbour.'

'Thanks...and sorry, especially when you're just trying to be a saint.'

Patrick's smile widened. 'It's not the first time that's been said about me.' He winked.

I laughed. 'Right.'

'So where are you staying anyway?'

For someone I'd just met, this guy was certainly asking a lot of questions. But he hadn't forced the issue when I'd refused his offer of a lift, which made me more inclined to trust him. Besides, I did need some info.

'I haven't sorted any accommodation out yet. I was going to wing it,' I said. 'I don't suppose you know anywhere to stay near Skara Brae?'

Patrick's eyes tightened on me for a fraction of second. 'Ah, the archaeological tourist hotspot.'

'That's the one.'

'But not normally so popular in the winter.'

I shrugged. 'I've come all this way especially to see it.'

'Any particular reason?'

God, this guy was nosey. I needed to shut this conversation down. Time to throw in my cover story. 'I'm writing a thesis about Skara Brae being the forerunner to Stonehenge.'

Patrick's brown eyes peered into mine like he knew I wasn't telling him the truth. 'Older than the pyramids, they say.'

'Yes...'

'No other reason then?'

Oh, Patrick so knew the real reason I was here. After all, I wouldn't be the first. The UFO boards had been filled with reports of the investigators who'd already come out here to study the outbreak of strange symbols that had been appearing all over Orkney. People were already saying it was the latest form of crop circles, another phenomenon I'd been sceptical about initially.

If you had told me a year back that I would one day know everything about crop circles, I would have laughed in your face. But that was the old Lauren. The new version of me, the one standing on a freezing ferry, was a completely different woman.

Patrick tipped his head to one side, still waiting for my

answer. 'I'm pursuing my research into Skara Brae,' I said, trying to sound convincing.

'I see...'

I could tell by the way his expression stiffened almost imperceptibly that Patrick thought I was lying. Not that it mattered. Everyone had their secrets, although mine were bigger than most.

Patrick gazed out towards Orkney with a faraway look in his eyes. Together we watched a bird, possibly a gannet, dive into the surf. A moment later it surfaced with a silver fish trapped in its beak. Patrick finally turned back to me.

'I can recommend a wonderful pub with the cosiest rooms not too far from there. The Guillemot. Great seafood and –' he tapped his flask – 'plenty more of this there too, including some from a fine fifteen-year-old cask.'

I laid on my best winning smile for him. 'That all sounds great.'

'Grand stuff. Just tell the taxi driver the Guillemot and they'll know the way. But my offer of a lift still stands.'

'Thanks, but no. I'm sure you understand.'

'I do... Like I said, sad times.'

'They are...' I gave him an apologetic smile as the ferry started to turn towards the harbour now visible in the distance.

'I'd better get back to my car. We'll be landing soon,' Patrick said. 'Anyway, nice to meet you, lass. I hope your research goes well.'

'Thanks. And thank you for introducing me to Highland Park.'

He smiled. 'Any time.' He nodded to me and then headed to the doorway.

Behind the ferry, thunderous black clouds were beginning to roll in towards the island. The forecast had mentioned something about a big storm on the way.

Rain started to patter down, rapidly intensifying. I drew my jacket in tighter round myself.

As the ferry slid towards the harbour, I grabbed my rucksack from the seat where I'd left it and prayed I wasn't chasing another dead end.

To continue the story and buy Earth Song, book one in the Earth Song series, just click on the link below. However, do please leave that oh so precious review on the next page before you go. https://geni.us/EarthSongSeries

Printed in Great Britain
by Amazon